T

## Fiction

After Jessica — money and a girl gone missing
Hitman Sam — a trainee hitman and love triangle
One for the Road — a hit-and-not-run novel
Oh, Henry — a comic dog-detective*
Henry Short Stories – comic dog-detective shorts*
The Serial Dater — 31 dates in 31 days*
The Serial Dieter — 31 dishes in 31 days*
*published as Rachel Cavanagh

*Short Story Collections*
Shorts — a collection of short short stories
Flashes — a collection of shorter short stories

## Non-Fiction

*Morgen Bailey's Creative Writing Workbooks*

Writer's Block Workbooks
1000+ exercises and 50+ tips per book

Editing Fiction ~ A Writer's Guide
Morgen's guide to writing a story then pulling it apart

**Shorts**

A Collection of Short Short Stories

ISBN no. 978-1-913633-14-1



Published in 2020 by August Publishing UK.



www.augustpublishing.co.uk

Cover design by Caroline Vincent.

Thank you for purchasing this book.

If you found this book useful, please encourage your friends to purchase their own copy.

# Shorts

## Short Short Stories

~

Morgen Bailey

This collection contains 82 stories of 500 words and over. All these pieces were originally published in the 'Story and Day May' and 'Fifty 5pm' collections, written from prompts provided by www.storyaday.org or from Morgen's imagination, re-edited for this edition.

We have crimes afoot, characters with and without friends, loves lost and found, homages, heroes and zeros, humans and non-humans, ghosts and a werewolf. With stories in first, second and third-person points of view, the characters shop, work, or go on journeys, some not beyond their own four walls.

I enjoyed writing them and hope you enjoy reading them.

**Morgen**

## Waiting for the Number Twelve

"You're new," Sylvia said, shuffling and sitting more upright on the bench.

The man smiled.

Sylvia looked up to the sky then back at the man. "Not so hot today."

The man nodded.

Sylvia wasn't used to people not talking to her, so she tried again. "Are you waiting for the number twelve?"

"I am," he said. "You?"

She wasn't sure why she was there but it definitely wasn't for the number twelve. Her birthday was on the twelfth so she'd remember. Maybe that was why she'd asked him. It seemed the natural thing to do. Realising he'd asked her the same question, sort of, Sylvia shook her head.

"Oh?" The man raised his bushy eyebrows.

He reminded her of Denis Healey except this man, her man until the number twelve arrived, was thinner. Just as young but blue, Sylvia thought, his eyes were bluer. She couldn't remember what colour Denis's eyes actually were, there was a lot she couldn't remember these days, but she didn't think they were ever like his… her man.

He sneezed and pulled out a not-quite-eye-blue cotton handkerchief, more royal, like King George wears.

"Bless you," Sylvia said timidly but unsure why. Suddenly she couldn't remember how old she was, or what month it was, and began to panic.

"Are you alright?" her man asked.

"Oh," she said, flustered, but his voice was so soothing that she was already relaxing. "Thirty-seven."

"Sorry?"

"I don't know."

"It's okay," he said, and put a hand on her arm.

"I think I'm waiting for the thirty-seven." Or was she thirty-seven?

"Oh," he said.

Sylvia thought he looked like a John. She had a John once but she knew she didn't have him anymore. Someone had told her that once and it stuck. So 'her man' became John. "Where does the number twelve go?"

"Excuse me?"

"Your bus. Where does it go?"

"Erm," John hesitated. "The town centre."

"That's a shame."

"Really?"

"I thought it might go somewhere nice, like the beach or…"

The man laughed.

Sylvia screwed up her nose and felt like the rabbit from Alice in Wonderland, or Tabitha in Bewitched. She wanted to twitch her nose to see if anything magical happened but she knew real life wasn't like that.

"Are you going to work?" she asked the man.

He nodded.

"You look very smart."

"Thank you."

She liked his uniform, green instead blue like her first John's, more hospital than navy. It was reassuring.

Sylvia winced as a drop of rain hit her nose. "It's raining."

"Oh dear," the man said, holding out his right hand, palm side upwards.

"I didn't bring an umbrella," Sylvia continued. "I hope the bus won't be long."

"Maybe we should find somewhere to shelter."

"That's a good idea."

"Shall we?" the man said, looping his left arm into her right.

Sylvia looked at his arm, then up at him and smiled.

As Jason Evans led his oldest resident back into the nursing home foyer, he smiled, knowing that tomorrow, he'd be sitting on the garden bench next to Sylvia Tyler, pretending to wait for the number twelve bus.

## An English Summer

Sheltering from the storm under the old oak tree, you look up and try to find a break in the grey cloud. The harder you look the more you realise there's no shading; it's all one colour, like photocopy paper for bland posters about bland events.

And that reminds you of Eric. And why you left him. He'd been the fun one at the beginning, pulling you to places you hadn't wanted to go, until he'd stopped pulling and settled in Hull. Dull Hull. He'd laughed and said it could have been worse, that it could have been Corby, but at least you knew people in Corby.

You'd weathered each other these past ten years, outgrowing him as you'd become outgoing, going out with friends from the gym and the writing group.

He'd had his bowling club but then they'd laughed at him, an innocent laugh, and he vowed never to return. With no interest in writing or getting fit, he'd refused your invitations, so stayed at home and vegetated.

And it had been like that until you'd woken up one morning, looked at him and realised there was nothing. No passion. No laughter. No happy ever after. And you'd wanted more.

So you'd packed, and gone to live with one of the poets; Sadie. And you'd begun to laugh again. And so had your writing. Dark tales turned to humour and you'd watched the glint in Sadie's eyes as you read them to her.

Until last week, when Eric had turned up. Full of fury, full of the passion that had been missing, but he'd got it all wrong… she was just a friend, a colleague of the arts.

He'd pushed you aside, into the bannister, winded you and you'd sat down… for a moment to catch your breath.

Sadie and Eric had argued, about you, but you hadn't wanted that attention. So you went through to the kitchen where Sadie was making the dinner and watched, in slow motion, as Eric grabbed the knife from her hand and plunged it into her heart. The heart that had been full of compassion for a stray, for you.

He'd been full of remorse, after the event, but it was too late. Too late to explain.

And now as the rain falls, you watch them lower the coffin, look over at Sadie's husband Ronan and their two children, and you want to say “sorry” again. For the hundredth time. But all you can think of is that it’s summer, that it should be warm, that you should be wearing a skimpy dress, with Sadie reading poetry to you, clinking glasses of Pimms.

As Ronan throws earth into the hole, you feel a tug at your wrist and look round. The man in the navy uniform tells you it’s time to go. He gives you a kind smile, as if he’s *on* your side as well as being *by* your side. You take one last look back at Ronan. He nods as you’re led away to start the life sentence for killing the man who’d killed his wife.

## Two Backwards, One Forwards

Rafferty had never saved a life before. He wasn't even sure this really qualified – the paramedics had taken over pretty quickly but he'd been the one who'd dragged the woman from the pool, lain her down and put her in the recovery position, something he'd not done since scouts, and back then Heath Wingate hadn't counted as someone in any danger.

Rafferty hoped the woman would forgive him for chopping off her hair. He'd not been the first one to spot her but the only one with scissors. If it hadn't been for Maya's insistence that he mend her doll's dress, he'd not have had them with him.

"I'll do it when we get back, Maya," he'd said.

"I want to take her with me."

"But you'll be swimming."

"You won't be, so it'll give you something to do."

When had his six-year old daughter become such an adult? he wondered. Since her mother had died. Now he had both roles: father – breadwinner; mother – nurturer. He was better at the former. More practice: nine years vs. eighteen months.

When you go to work, kiss your wife goodbye, as you do every day, stroke the side of her face as something had compelled Rafferty to do that morning, you expect her to be there when you get home, laughing and joking.

You don't expect a call from the school asking why no one's collected your daughter, regular as clockwork, only Louisa's clock had stopped ticking – just like that – as if the battery had run out. Two hearts, two batteries: Louisa's and their unborn son's. Two lives he'd been unable to save.

A year and a half later, there he was, sitting by a Spanish pool in the summer's early morning warmth – an only parent to an only child. A happy one, on the outside.

Maya's screaming had jolted him out of a doze. Not quite asleep. Only eyes closed. Resting, if anyone had asked. Too little sleep for both of them. Nightmares – shared subconscious.

The sewing kit and tiny dress had scattered onto the cobalt blue tiles as he'd bolted off the lounger and run to where Maya stood pointing at a figure two metres underwater, hair trapped in the drain, costume sparkling like a mermaid. He'd gone back for the scissors, panicking when he couldn't find them, then spotting them under a neighbouring empty lounger, he'd straddle-jumped into the pool.

He'd felt guilty, cutting the woman's beautiful auburn hair with the pathetic travel-size blades until she came loose and started floating to the top. He swam up after her, grabbed her, towed her by her chin, arm across her chest, as he'd been taught.

She'd been lighter than he imagined she should be. Slim. Pretty. Louisa-esque.

He'd felt a pulse, and as he watched the stretcher being taken to the ambulance, he was sure there'd been a hint of a smile.

## Life in the Old Dog

Condoms. Why are there condoms in your handbag? You look at the outside again to make sure it's your bag. You knew it was when you opened it and the rest of the contents are yours, but these certainly aren't.

Your mind races for clues. The only other person to go near the bag was Cliff and he'd have no use for condoms. As far as you're aware he's never cheated on you and anyway, he's so short-sighted and deaf he'd never notice or hear if anyone was… what's the phrase the youngsters use today?... 'hitting on' him.

You're always so fastidious about leaving your bag unattended, ever since being cautioned at the airport when Cliff took you to Paris for your fortieth wedding anniversary. Not cautioned, he'd say, warned, but it felt like they were the police, with their starched uniforms and polished shoes.

Today, the only time you went out was to go to the supermarket then the garage for petrol. You'd filled the trolley while Cliff sat in the café then you'd filled the car with unleaded while he queued to pay. Then he'd thrown the receipt and some chocolate in your bag. The chocolate you'd picked out when you'd got home, put it to one side on top of the washing machine while he parked the car in the garage, and that's when you'd found the condoms.

The receipt, you remember, will explain all. Petrol… chocolate… condoms. So it was Cliff. You look up to the ceiling to avoid the tears you know you want to cry, but you won't give him the satisfaction. You know he's not bought them for you, you stopped having babies years ago, so if they're not for you…

The threat of tears turns to welling anger, and you have your arms crossed when he walks back into the kitchen.

"The garage door's rather squeaky. Could do with a bit of WD-40 but seems I've run out. Could you remind…"

You say nothing, just stare at him, the washing machine, then back at him.

He looks as innocent as the day you met. He turns back to you, a frown crinkling his normally smooth forehead. "What, dear?"

His eyes follow yours as you turn from him again to the

contents on top of the washing machine and he smiles. “Oh yes… Fancy some?”

Your scowl softens to a frown so he continues. “Chocolate? It’s Fruit & Nut, your favourite.”

“And these?” You hold up the packet of condoms.

“I know,” he says. “I’ve tried giving up. I didn’t think you’d mind if I only got a pack of ten.”

“Ten?”

“I’ll make them last. I chose a different brand to normal.”

“Normal!”

“These are supposed to be better for you.”

You’re about to throw them at him when he continues. “Low tar.”

“What?”

“Cigarettes. I shouldn’t, I know.”

“These aren’t cigarettes, Clifford!”

“Aren’t they?”

“No, Clifford. These are condoms.”

“They are? Why did she give me condoms?”

You burst out laughing at his pained expression, like the little boy you remember from school.

Cliff winks, takes your hand and leads you upstairs.

## Two Rows

As you wait for her to get on the bus, you wonder for the umpteenth time whether she's married. She talks in first person. Always I, never we. Singular. No ring, like you. You've never spoken to her, of course, only heard snippets of conversation from two rows ahead, lower than you. You're two steps up, which feels a little godlike, not that you've ever considered yourself any kind of god.

You think you love her, sure of it; you've never felt this way before, not even for… Almost every morning for the past three years you've seen her, evenings too sometimes; strokes of luck that have you both finishing at the same time.

You don't know where she works as she turns left as she gets off the bus, you right. You've thought about turning left, following her, but that would be creepy and you don't want to do anything that would put her off. Not that you've done anything to encourage her.

She knows you exist, sees you when she walks up the aisle to her seat, but not how much of an existence it is: work, sleep, little 'play' in between.

She's always smiling, chatting to fellow passengers… on the phone, never to you. But then you don't let her get that close. Closeness is something you struggle with. Have done since…

You don't like to think of back then. You'd rather this be a blank canvas on which to paint happy thoughts, fondly-remembered places, warm embraces.

She's late this morning. You only remember her being late twice before – other than being on holiday. But then she didn't turn up at all. You'd known she was going away – Mrs Ellison had told you, because the two ladies talk. A lot. Just day-to-day stuff, nothing too personal, more mother-to-daughter conversations.

Then you notice Mrs Ellison's shoulders moving, and you catch flashes of a red handkerchief with a white embroidered 'F.E.'. You don't know her first name and that sets your mind racing. Fiona? Frances? Probably something old school like Florence. Your Mrs Nightingale.

You've never seen her cry before, Mrs Ellison, and you've known her longer than Beth. Just the thought of her name makes you smile but then you see Mrs Ellison turn to look at you and she bursts into tears.

You leave your seat and sit in the empty one beside her – Beth's seat. You'll keep it warm until she arrives. There are still people getting on, so she has time.

You want to put your arm around her… Mrs Ellison. Tell her it can't be that bad and you're still debating when she takes your hands in hers and speaks, between sobs.

"Oh… Evan."

You wonder if her tears are because of Mr Ellison, but you don't think he's ever done something to warrant this. She doesn't say any more and you wonder if she's waiting for you to speak but she lets go of your hand and picks up a newspaper from her lap. She unfolds it, revealing the front page. You recognise the photograph. The smile.

You feel sick as you read the text. 'Local secretary, Beth Munroe, killed in freak accident.'

The bus lurches and starts its journey. To the town centre. To the bus stop where you'll be getting off, turning right, as you make your way to the bank.

## Being Weird Together

It wasn't until she overheard a conversation that Lollie had ever considered herself weird. That was the word they'd used. She wasn't very good at long words but she knew the funny ones, the weird ones.

"Weird, strange, per-cue-lee-er," she said, thinking it great to be called any of those. 'Nice' is boring. 'Sweet' is what an old aunt calls you. And in half an hour hers would be looking after her while her mum and dad went out. To the cinema.

Lollie wanted to go with them but they said she was too young. She was always too young, unless her mother wanted her to do something, like go to the corner shop to fetch Auntie Minnie's favourite sweets; barley sugar.

Lollie had tried one once and thought it tasted like medicine, so had spat it onto her hand, and Auntie Minnie had told her off.

"Lauren!" she'd said, never calling her Lollie. "You're named after a famous actress," she'd said once, "not an ice cream."

But Lollie loved ice creams, especially cherry, apricot or mint with tiny chocolate chip flakes, or all three. And always in a cone, never in one of those cardboard tubs that go warm and soggy if you take too long to eat.

It was while she was waiting in the queue for a hundred grams from one of the jars behind the counter that she'd heard the boys talking about her. She'd turned round and realised they went to the same school. Achim something, Bradley Sutton, and a third she didn't recognise. "That Lollie's weird," the third boy said and she wondered how he knew if she didn't know him. The other two had laughed and agreed.

She wanted to go home – she didn't want them to see her, but she knew Aunt Minnie had eaten all the barley sugar's last time she'd visited and would expect there to be some so Lollie had no choice.

She was only small and the man behind her was huge so as long as he stayed there, and the boys took longer in the corner of the shop than she did getting served, they might not see her.

She should be getting back home before her aunt arrived, but Lollie waited outside the shop until the boys came out. Feeling brave, she wanted to speak to them, ask them what they had meant.

Achim came out first eating a packet of crisps, then Bradley, pouring some Smarties onto his palm and throwing them into his mouth, tipping his head back.

Despite it being cold and almost dark, the third boy came out unwrapping an ice cream.

"I thought you didn't like those," Achim said.

"Weird, you called it," Bradley added.

The other boy nodded. "I know but it's like Marmite. Sometimes you hate it and sometimes…"

So they hadn't meant her. She felt a little disappointed but it had made her think about herself and she liked being weird, even if for only a few minutes, so she decided she would stay weird and if her aunt didn't like it, that was too bad. Maybe if the boy Lollie didn't know liked weird, they could be weird together.

## Wreckage

Jamie stood in the wreckage of his ransacked house, trying to take it all in.

He didn't even know where to start. Was there a start?

He had to call the police, he knew that, but on this side of the city, it was a fairly regular occurrence so he also knew the chances of catching anyone, of them being stupid enough to leave any fingerprints, was slim, but he had to for insurance purposes.

Insurance. "Sh–!" Wasn't it due around now?

He went to the kitchen, put on a pair of yellow Marigold washing-up gloves then bolted up the stairs to the back bedroom.

He looked at the bookcase but it was empty, the files scattered across the floor. He searched through them, the fact they were all the same shade of blue adding to his frustration.

When he found the right one, he clasped it to his chest, went to the landing phone and dialled 999.

The mess in the spare room had been more than enough so instead of checking on the other rooms: the bathroom, his bedroom, he returned downstairs. He'd deal with whatever faced him once the police had been and gone. He'd have to leave everything as it was anyway, in case they did take it seriously and bring a photographer.

His camera. He'd bought a lovely new red Nikon only the week before for a class he'd enrolled on. Had it come with insurance? Knowing his luck…

After filling the kettle, he opened the folder on the kitchen table. The reminder letter from Wickett & Pringle lay on the top. Jamie scanned the text then found the renewal date; seventeenth July. It was the nineteenth. The annual premium had gone up so they'd not automatically taken the payment from his bank account but had instructed him to ring to renew and 'we would only be too glad to assist'. No chance they would do so now.

Jamie slumped in the chair and hung his head over the paperwork. He stuck out his tongue and blew a half-hearted raspberry.

He hadn't expected a rapid response to his 999 call but had only just made himself a cup of tea, surprisingly difficult to do while wearing washing-up gloves, when he saw the flashing blue light outside.

He opened the front door as two officers approached it. He then spotted the ambulance.

"Are you the home owner?" the taller of the two asked. Jamie read the officer's name badge. Wade.

Jamie nodded. "I only called the police. I didn't ask for an ambulance."

"Step inside, please, sir," Wade ordered.

Jamie took a step back.

"All the way, please," his colleague, Rylett, added.

Jamie reached the lounge doorway, still facing the officers. "I don't understand. What's going on?"

"Where's the woman?" Wade asked, dropping the 'sir'.

"What wo–?"

"Never mind. Rylett, you look upstairs. I'll stay down here with Mr…"

"Dawson. Jamie Dawson. But…" He watched Rylett go upstairs then Wade ushered Jamie into the lounge.

Wade tilted his chin towards the mess that was surrounding them. "So, Mr Dawson. Domestic or were you looking for something?"

"No. Neither. I've been out, only just got in. I don't know… what woman? Who–?"

But before he could continue, Rylett appeared. "She's up there. We're too late."

"What?" Jamie asked as Wade strapped cuffs to his gloved hands.

## Without Knowing

You've never seen her so happy. You wish you knew her name, to be brave enough to ask. She looks as if she wouldn't mind, but she doesn't look in your direction for long enough.

Like you, she always sits in the same seat, same departure, same destination until she turns left, you right at the station exit. Different clothes but same shoes. Hers are black high-gloss high heels that make you ever so slightly horny… no, childlike, the years strip away every time you see her.

You figure she's nearing retiring age, maybe three or four years older than you at most.

She doesn't wear a wedding ring but you think she has children. You're not sure why but she looks the type; homely, kind, with no weight on her shoulders other than maybe that of the responsibility of looking after a young grandchild. Widowed… or divorced, for a while, like you.

You'd like to take her on your boat, her whole family, go away for a weekend, somewhere like the Norfolk Broads where it's flat. Or play something to her on your Steinway when you're alone with her, after a nice meal or the theatre.

You don't dress to match your wealth but she doesn't strike you as the sort of person to care, not about money, only the important things like family and love.

It's why you travel by train, a car too lonely, even with a chauffeur. You tried it for a while but it wasn't you, your newfound wealth comfortable yet uncomforting.

You can barely remember what it feels like to be in love. You've been doing well lately, not dwelling, and she's been helping. Without knowing, she's your Samaritan, just seeing her gives you something to think about as you sit behind your desk on the twentieth floor of your new high-rise office.

Your stop is coming up, and you start to dread the next seventy-two hours, a weekend without the train journeys, without her. Not seeing her between Friday and Monday mornings. Never the evenings, only your starts coinciding.

You go to stand and she reaches out for the handrail, skin missing skin by an inch or two.

"Sorry," she says, but there's no apology needed. "You work at McCardie's, don't you," she adds.

You want to say something but that will give away your accent, that you *are* McCardie, so you just nod.

"I work for the opposition," she says, and you know she means Cohen & Sons.

Before you can stop yourself, you laugh, and she smiles, her green eyes luminescent.

The train stops and you signal for her to go first. She bows her head and you follow her off the train.

You both walk in silence, following the crowd like sheep, until you get to the exit, out into fresher air.

Instead of going left, she stops, steps aside, turns and faces you, waits for everyone else to pass. You want to go right, head for your office, but your feet won't move.

She holds out her hand. "Faith Cohen. Arlo was my husband. He dressed just like you. Quiet too."

## Surrounded By It In Life, Surrounded In Death

Colin thought it would have been sorted by now. How hard was it to pick a bunch of flowers?

"The blue ones are nice," he offered.

Miriam shook her head. "Papa never liked blue."

*All men like blue*, Colin thought. *What's not to like*?

"It's cold," Miriam said, as if reading his mind. "Papa wasn't like that."

All the years Colin had known Jeremiah Sawyer, Colin had never seen a warm side to him and now Colin had to wait patiently while his wife chose the accompaniment to the old man's coffin. Colin would have had him sent off in a cardboard box if they'd had one big enough.

"The best that money can buy," he heard her say as she pointed to a picture in a display folder.

The undertaker bowed his head but Colin was sure there was a hint of a smile. He imagined the man rubbing his hands together had they not been holding the folder.

"Wise choice, madam," he said.

Colin thought it patronising but said nothing. As long as Miriam was happy, he was happy – he knew how to have an easy life, but of course she wasn't.

Colin watched as the man clapped the book shut, making Miriam jump, then he pulled out another folder, a red one this time.

*Oh great*, Colin thought as a sea of two-dimensional coffins was thrust before her. He looked at the prices; increasing as she worked her way through the folder.

"He's going to be scattered anyway, isn't he?" Colin grimaced when he realised he'd said it out loud.

Miriam and the undertaker, whose name Colin had forgotten as soon as the man had brought out the first folder, the 'Manager' badge not helping, both glared at him.

"Sorry," Colin whimpered.

"Papa deserves the best," Miriam sobbed and accepted the offering of a marble-enclosed box of tissues from the 'Manager'.

"Sorry, Miriam," Colin repeated. "Of course he does." Colin sat in silence while Miriam flicked pages back and forth.

"He liked walnut," Colin finally blurted out.

Miriam turned round to face him. "What?"

"His car has a walnut dash. He must have liked it."

The undertaker leaned forward and turned a couple of pages of the folder then tapped one of the coffins.

Miriam turned back to the desk. "Walnut… That *is* nice. Okay. Let's have that one."

As his wife handed over their joint credit card, Colin smiled as he recalled the conversation he and Jeremiah had had not long after he'd bought the car. How much Jeremiah had loved everything about it except for what he'd called the 'revolting walnut dash'.

Surrounded by it in life, surrounded in death.

## Under

Feeling a little under the weather, I plod along with my dog. It's raining so he's less than enthusiastic, I completely understand. We'd normally go to the park, let him loose to play in the undergrowth but being underwhelmed by the clouds, we take a shortcut through the underpass, as the underground train rumbles overhead.

I imagine how jaded the drivers must be, repetition the height of boredom – smiling like an undertaker at anyone who catches their eye.

I prefer to drive, points A to B, and growl at those who hog the motorway's middle lane, me wishing it were legal to undertake.

My new lodger has plans to visit somewhere different in the UK every weekend, an escape from an ex – so far under the thumb she was paper-thin, him being underhand at the best of times.

He misunderstands two women living together, under the same roof, enjoys undermining our confidence when he's under the influence. Alcohol is the devil to some, a solace to others.

"He's a decent man… underneath it all," she says, but I know the undercurrent of what *he* says and stay robust like an underpinned house.

She's also talking of writing her autobiography, of her life in the circus and everywhere in between. I'm more of a contemporary fiction writer, history being my worst subject at school – researching undergarments of the elite and their relationship with the underclass holding little appeal.

Unlike my adult life, I was an underachiever at secondary school, underperforming… like a council I know, spending too much money on a new building with a too-small underground car park.

We're off to see two movies today, my lodger and I, both chick flicks, more my cup of English Breakfast than sci-fi or fantasy, although I did enjoy the Underworld series with Kate Beckinsale, a much underrated actress but then she's British, we're used to being the underdog.

Lodger number two arrives soon and I have my work cut out; do some painting… a bit of undercoat here and there, under the purple and blue that my house exudes. Things will have to change when he arrives, the man of the house, we'll have to hide our underwear after the weekly wash. I've seen photos of him and he looks a little underweight, rectified I'm sure once he's under my wing.

I should be editing my early novels but I'm waiting for my first readers to submit their comments on the third one, underline things that don't make sense. One of my betas is an actor, an understudy sometimes, and his grammar is faultless so his alterations are never undervalued.

In the meantime I have jobs to do, the house needing attention before our third party arrives… the bathroom floor tiles to be removed and replaced over underlay so the uneven floorboards don't crack them anymore. Given the time I have, I think I may have underestimated the work to be done.

So with notepad tucked discreetly under my arm, I head under the house to check my DIY store… I may be some time…

## Over

"Over," I say, and my dog and I cross the road. Overnight, after oversleeping, I've become overcome with cold. I'm usually overrun with chores but I'm taking it easy today. A contrast to yesterday, blitzing my overgrown garden; now my pavement is overcrowded with overfilled brown wheelie bins and strong green gardening bags.

I look in the dictionary and have never heard of 'overhand'. Wikipedia tells me it's a boxing term and a knot, and I'm not a violent person but right now I'm angry. My neighbour's extension has gone over and above what was promised to me; it's already overhanging the light into my south-facing garden.

I head to the bank to check that I'm not overdrawn, not dipped into my overdraft, then buy some over-the-counter medicine before this cold overpowers me. I think I've been overcharged. On the way home, another neighbour calls me over. So, switching off my iPod's classical overture, we talk over the fence, while his England flag flutters overhead.

To say I'm fat is an overstatement. I'm a little overweight and could do with an overhaul of my eating habits, but it would be an oversimplification to say five-a-day fruit and veg would do it. I often overlook them at the supermarket, an unhealthy oversight. My body's been doing a bit too much overtime so it really wouldn't hurt.

An early night is also long overdue but I have plans tonight (I'm having writing friends over) so an afternoon nap will have to make do.

My back is complaining, it does that a lot. When I go to pick something up it says, "don't overdo it" but I never listen. Tomorrow morning I shall carry stacks of Red Cross donated books which I'll tip on to the counter and their shiny covers will slip against each other and overbalance on to the floor.

In the afternoon, what energies I have will be used to empty my loft (pre-electrician's visit), bring down the boxes of already-bought presents that will overwhelm my mother in September, when she's easily pleased, although I suspect she overplays it, oversells for my benefit. My aunt, her twin, will just look overawed, carrying her overladen gift bag into the kitchen, putting her Andre Rieu DVDs with the others. An überfan.

Then Wednesday lunchtime my job sharer will read me her handover notes as our shifts overlap, my turn to work two and a half days before another weekend arrives.

I usually travel overseas but my friend and I are busy so we'll wait a year. She's off to Mexico, to visit family, me to a writers' conference at Winchester. I've never been there before so I'll need to pay attention so I don't overshoot the junction, overstep the mark on the map for the venue.

If I played cricket I think it would be underarm not overarm, that's just how I throw; like a girl.

Radio Litopia's Agent Pete calls me an overachiever but I like to think I'm just overjoyed with all things literary. We chat during Sunday night's Open House then our Skype connection is terminated before I overstay my welcome. I live and breathe writing, albeit stuffily through a red overblown nose. I sneeze over and over again.

Having over-egged today's prompt, this ditty is over. Well, anymore would be overkill, wouldn't it?

## The Case That Sherlock Couldn't Crack

Being named after a famous figure from history was always going to weigh heavily on my shoulders. Sherlock. I mean, who these days calls their kid Sherlock? Maybe back in the sixties. Okay, point taken.

You see my parents were fans of literature and they had everything that Sir Arthur had written; signed first editions included. I was torn when they died as to what to do with them. The books, that is, not my parents.

I had a choice: keep them, let them gather dust, and work full-time or sell them and live comfortably. Yes, you can guess what I did. Besides, with them filling almost every bookcase in the house, it meant I wasn't tripping over stuff. Okay, slight exaggeration but I like a lived-in-but-neat-and-tidy existence, plus submitting stories to competitions doesn't come cheap. Yeah, I'm a literature fan too.

What I hadn't expected going through it all was finding Sir Arthur's journals. All handwritten, and signed. Bit egotistical if you ask me – like he knew they'd be worth something one day. Maybe they already were. Who knows? Sir Arthur, I suppose.

I must admit I did get rather excited when I found them, stuffed rather irreverently in an old shoe box. I say 'old' but not as old as the journals. Nineteen fifties, judging by the brand, lettering etc. Felt a bit like a detective myself. Figure my namesake would have been proud.

Anyway, these journals were a bit of a shock. Didn't think my parents had been that wealthy, being one-offs and all that.

Then the biggest shock was when I sat down and read them. Took me a while, a few days actually, and… I still can't believe it even now.

That Sherlock had a child. With Irene Adler. I did think at the time "why didn't she tell him?" but then felt stupid because they're just fictional characters. Then I started putting two and two together, and it made me wonder why Sir Arthur had written it in the journals but then not acted on it.

You know, written another story about it. He wasn't Sherlock's biggest fan, he'd tried to kill him off, so this bit of unwed scandal would have been easy. Up the ratings as well for sure.

So I did a bit of digging online. The internet in the nineties wasn't as forthcoming as it would be now, so I didn't find anything. But then I wouldn't, would I? They were only in his journals.

But I wondered why he'd put anything at all. It wasn't until I re-read those passages that a pattern started forming, like a coded message. Now I knew Sherlock would have been proud of me. Well, probably not given the circumstances, especially if he didn't know he was a dad.

But when I'd finally worked it out, there it was in black and white. A name. Sherlock's love child, I think Sir Arthur's too… Irene, same name as Miss Adler… same as my grandmother.

## All Heart

The surgeon had told you that you shouldn't feel any different after the operation. Uncomfortable, yes, but you're not sure what you are feeling. Elated? Strong. Youthful. Not how you'd expected but then you'd spent years feeling sub-human, on enough pills to be a walking Tic-Tac packet, so anything else would have been better. And this, whatever it is, is beyond that.

Someone remarks on your lack of visitors, of family. Not loudly but just enough for you to catch it.

Angus, next door, has so many relatives that they have your allocation of chairs, and the almost-constant chatter is enough company when you need it. Angus's had a bypass, just like you, but he's not taking it so well. Or rather, it:him.

You're due to be discharged today, soon in fact, you're dressed, bag packed, just waiting for the all-clear but you're in no hurry and you listen in on the conversations around you, from both sides; Angus on your right and Elvis on your left. You know that's not his real name, you've not caught that yet as he's a new recruit to the Thompson Ward, but all he hums is The King so you've pretended it's him; with your eyes shut, curtain closed.

As the doctor approaches your bed, you smile, sit up straight and shake his hand when he offers it. He asks you how you're doing and you say you've never felt better. You mean every word and you're glad you don't have to lie any more. You want to start over, go back to your bedsit and look forward. Stop dwelling on things you can't change. So you sign the discharge papers and leave.

It's a ten-minute walk, past the park and normally that's all you'd do, go past, but today you want to stop, go in, go to the lake, watch the dogs chasing the geese, the children feeding the ducks. Watch your old life but without regret.

You have pocket change so you head for the café to see it all from behind the warmth of the glass. You'll buy some chips, hot, salted, unketchuped. They'll be washed down with a large mug of tea, sweet and strong like Clara said you were. In the early days.

Today feels like an early day and you don't mind that it's cold. Not really. The freshness feels inviting, crisp, but you've skipped breakfast so you'd rather eat here than at home.

As you approach the large panoramic window you see that the café's packed, but figure you can probably squeeze in somewhere. You're not as big as you used to be.

As you head for the door, you see a young woman struggling with a pushchair. You lunge forward, grabbing the door handle and pull it open, waving her in with a dramatic sweeping gesture.

"Thanks," she says in a broad local accent. "You're all heart."

You smile and let the door close after her. You watch her take the last seat and you head for the lake.

## I Could Have Cried

"Stop doing that!"

I'd lost count of how many times I'd told my sister to stop kicking the counter.

It was bad enough I was there cashing in my giro – that's what my gran calls it – I'm unemployed, unemployable my sister says, but she still wasn't paying any attention. '

Selective hearing' my mum used to say, but we'd been to the doctor so I knew she could hear as well as I could.

"Elaine, do that one more time and I'll–" and that's when I saw him, so I changed lanes, his was the longest but it was no surprise.

And all women except for old Mr Rogers and I didn't mind being behind him as I meant I got to see 'him'. He was new.

'Him', not Mr Rogers. I was ignoring Eleanor by now which she didn't like but I didn't care.

I did wish I'd put on something pretty instead of my dungarees. And when he wasn't looking, I pulled the bow out of my hair. Bows are for children, aren't they.

I started making up names for him – he reminded me of Charlton Heston from that Ben Hur movie my dad loves, except 'he' had more clothes on… bummer.

But I imagined him all muscly and sweaty, and racing chariots around in circles with people cheering him on. I'd cheer for him. "Go on, Barry!" I'd say. Well, Charlton's a silly name, isn't it?

Then it was just Mr Rogers, me and 'him'. I stood left a bit so I could see over Mr Rogers' shoulders, and close enough to hear their conversation – boring of course – but his voice… Barry's not Mr Rogers', was sexy, like caramel, all dark and rich. He was dark too, like he'd been on the beach too long.

Then when Mr Rogers finally left, my heart thumped. I could see Barry's blue eyes up close.

I stepped forward, about to speak when he completely ignored me and pulled his blind down. 'Closed' it said, as if to rub it in.

Then I watched him walk behind his colleagues – that was back when the post office had more than one person serving – and head out the door… in my direction!

He smiled. I smiled. He brushed his hands through his lightly gelled hair. I wished I'd washed mine.

Then he opened his mouth to speak. "Hi," he said and I went to reply but saw he was looking through me. I turned round and saw my teacher, Mrs Eddison, smiling back at him.

Eddison. Mrs. Of course. She's married, only last month, not long back from her honeymoon. And Barry looks half her age.

Then they kissed right in front of me! I was going to say something but then Barry, or whatever his name is, he wasn't wearing a badge, said, "I love you, Mrs Eddison." I couldn't believe it so I stood there open-mouthed. Elaine was pulling at my dungarees but I still ignored her.

Then Mrs Eddison spoke. "I love you more, Mr Eddison."

I could have cried.

## Holding Her Hand

I can't bear it. It's been… oh God, six hours. That's not a good sign, is it. But she's alive. That's what matters. That's all that matters.

I hate hospitals. That's not strictly true. The last time I was… we were here, was when I gave birth to her. Six years ago. An hour a year. If they're another hour… please let them be another hour… let her see seven.

Ash was here then. Holding my hand while I screamed at him, calling him every name. You don't know what you're doing when you're… you know how it goes. Or not. Maybe you don't.

Oh God, please don't let me lose them both. I'll go to church again, I promise. You can't be that cruel twice. I'm sorry, I don't know what I'm saying.

Nurse! Please, is there any news? Thank you. I'd be grateful… very…

I don't know what I'd do if… No, mustn't think like that. She'll be fine. She has to be.

It's my fault. Well, not totally. I wasn't the one driving, speeding outside a school. Who does that? But I was late. A minute or two, that's all. Stayed to listen to the end of a play. Put it before her though, didn't I. Nothing's more important, I knew that. Know that.

If I'd been early, on time, the car wouldn't have been there yet. The road would have been clear when she'd chased the… Yes, it's the cat's fault. No, mine. We usually hold hands but I'd let go so she could say "hello". That's all, just a hello. How was I to know it was a scaredy… cat.

Of course the road may not have been clear – it's a school, but other drivers, parents, would have been going slower, legal, and they would have stopped. I hope they catch the son of a…

Oh no, he's walking towards me. He's taking his… what's it called? The surgical cap thing. No, no, no, no… Please don't say…

"Yes. That's me." I don't want to say anything else. I just want him to speak. Tell me quickly, get it over and done… one way or the other. Just say something. Why isn't he saying something? He must have done this hundreds of times.

Good news would be easy, quick. So it's… He's speaking. Just don't let him say, *We did everything we could* or *I'm sorry, Mrs Everett…*

I don't need every detail. It's too complicated.

"Please," I say out loud, "tell me. I can handle it." I've handled it before. Five years ago. Sudden, like this, couldn't be helped. Of course it could have. Everything can be helped but we knew the risks. You don't marry a policeman lightly.

Then the doctor tells me. Magic words: very slow recovery… will need your support… more operations.

I don't care what it takes. She's alive. Then it hits me; that her life has come full circle. Mine too. We'll both leave hospital not knowing what the future holds, but I know one thing for sure, she'll never be more loved and I'll be there… holding her hand, every step of the way.

## Gasping For Breath

As Woody stares through the fish tank, he wonders how long it'll be before the buzzer goes, before it's his turn to take the chair. He remembers his first visit to the dentist as a child. It's the needles he dreads the most. Always hated needles. And he can't see the point of the fish. Supposed to be therapeutic but seeing them going backwards and forwards or round in circles...

And what creature would want to swim in the residue of their food – and worse. If you can call it food. Looks more like confetti to him. It reminds him of his wedding to Sharon and now he knows how the fish feel.

Like them, he'd been oblivious to the pointlessness of it all. He just went with the flow, content with his life, sharing his abode with a creature that he thought he'd spend the rest of his life with.

Only she'd found a way out, a crack in the glass of their existence, and everything that his world had stood for cascaded down around him and he found himself fighting for air, unable to breathe as the enormity of his life hit him.

And that was what had led him here, to the room with the fish tank and the buzzer.

Looking around, he stares at a clock above his right shoulder. Almost midday. Ten minutes before the hands touch – a silent prayer.

He knows the chair waits for him on the other side of the door, and he grips the arms of the one he's sitting in now. Sitting sweating, unable to breathe again. But then he relaxes, resigned to the inevitable.

He looks at the other side of the room; the rows of people looking back at the fish tank, through it, at him. Some are wearing smiles, others scorn. Two standing wear uniforms with smug grins.

They've seen this scenario dozens of times, perhaps hundreds, and it's become a game to them; watch the needles, the plungers force the liquids, perfect measurements, a work of art.

One fish bobs to the surface and gasps for breath. Woody flinches as the buzzer goes.

A door to his left opens and a woman in white appears. Looking around the room, her gaze goes to the fish tank and she frowns at the gasping fish.

Putting her hand into her right pocket, she pulls out a notepad and pen and writes something down. She smiles at Woody and returns the notepad and pen to her pocket. She then looks at the other side of the room.

The frown reappears and she leans towards a coffee table, picks something up and points it at the wall.

“I’m sorry, Mr Riley,” she says as the prison scene is replaced with a cooking show. “It’s the receptionist’s warped sense of humour. Hooked on the crime channel, she is – they shouldn’t show that sort of thing on daytime TV.

I’ll speak to her again but she’s young. Anyway, do come this way. Dr Easton has everything ready. It won’t be as bad as you think. Don’t need so much these days. Count yourself lucky you’re not flying to Africa.”

## Biological Is All It Is

He says it was planted but you know better. Quentin's always been like that; a thief, a liar, a father to your child. Not a daddy. Biological is all it is but when he provides a roof over your heads, you can't say much.

You hold out the tea towel and he lays the dagger on it. Reverently as if it were a baby. Shows more respect to it than his own. Mia. The rosy pink cheeks nestled over rosy pink sheets.

You worry sometimes that she's too hot, too cold, but she's strong, stronger than you sometimes, and it scares you. Everything does these days.

You're not scared of him but the men he hangs around with. You've seen the looks they give Mia when they visit in the daytime. No jobs – you don't suppose they've ever had them.

"They make do," he says. Making do like he does, but it's never quite enough. You don't like asking for money but you know it's getting to that. Break the silence of the past year. Let your parents know that you're alright.

Some arguments you can't get over, and time doesn't heal in this case. It hurts, pulls apart, wounds… like a dagger. Like the dagger nestled in the discount store's blue and white check cotton. Buy one get one free, as most things are. The twins were until Thomas died just hours old… Quentin never forgave you for something beyond your control.

You spot a fleck on the blade and recoil, letting it drop to the floor.

Cloth and blade bounce and as the dagger hits the tiles, he hits you for being so stupid.

You don't recoil from that, you're used to it, like the silence at night when he doesn't bother to come home. You wish he'd stay away. You wish that one night you'd be brave enough to flee but you don't know if the other welcome would be any warmer.

"I'm going out," he announces as you go to pick the dagger and cloth off the floor.

You say nothing, just nod and smile the Geisha smile that hides beneath layers of make-up hiding the bruises.

As the front door slams, Mia starts crying and you feel like doing the same only you know the well is empty, a long time drained.

You pull two plastic bags from a green cotton holder, carefully wrap the dagger in one, then inside the cloth which you place into the second bag.

Going upstairs, you look in on Mia who has since gone quiet, though not asleep.

Pulling a suitcase from the top of the wardrobe you start packing; half Mia's, half yours, clothes barely big enough for her, yours that now drown you – the dagger beneath layers. You add a blanket, toy giraffe, then you pick up the phone and dial.

The taxi arrives quickly and you shut the front door, posting your keys through the letterbox.

The driver helps you strap Mia onto the back seat, next to you, then asks for the address as he shuts his door. You remain silent. When he asks you again, you take a deep breath and he starts to drive.

## Knew Better

Pandora knew better. She'd been told over and over. Only she thought she knew better. That it didn't matter. She'd been out to the ice-cream van a hundred times, probably more, but always hands clasped tightly to grandfather, grandmother, or mother. Never alone… 'til now.

It was a classic scenario. Hot summer's day, ice-cream van, little girls in school uniforms. A dream scenario to Hollis. He'd promised the judge he'd behave, told the parole board enough times so they believed him, but he knew better. They thought he knew better.

And there was this one little girl. She looked like a Patsy. He liked the name Patsy. Used to have a cat called Patsy, until his father took it away. Told him it had been run over but Hollis knew. His father looked guilty, for a second, long enough for Hollis to know.

He knew everything that his father did. And vowed never to be like him. But he couldn't escape. Just like the little girl who'd gone to his car to see the puppy, holding the ice-cream that had already started melting.

Except there was no puppy. He couldn't have pets after Patsy. Couldn't bear to let them go. He wouldn't let her go… this little girl in her navy blue and white uniform. So smart. With navy blue shoes and long white socks.

They had holes in them. Not old, like his socks, but symmetrical, like the middles of flowers. Hollis loved flowers. His mother would buy fresh ones every week until his father had lost his job and they'd run out of money.

But Hollis had plenty of money now. He'd look after Patsy like she was his flesh and blood. She'd forget, and call him "father". She'd be the sister he never had. The daughter he'd always wanted.

She knew it was wrong. “Don’t talk to strangers”, that’s what she’d been told. Except there was something familiar about him. He reminded her of her father. The little she could remember.

And his smile. He had a nice smile. Friendly. And she was in need of a new friend.

It had never been the same since they’d moved. So many times after her father had gone away. Her mother had promised that it would be fine, that there would be plenty of little girls for her to get on with, but she’d had that look in her eyes that Pandora had seen before.

Her mother had said that this was ‘it’ this time, that they’d stay, but Pandora knew better.

## Doing A Job I Love

It had felt a little odd. Being given something like this for doing a job I love. And you couldn't really call it that. Playing in a band a job? To receive an award for playing the drums was an added bonus. I'd been given a single drum, a cheap thing, when I was very young, my mum says two, but I think I was younger than that because I don't remember getting it, just it being there.

When my name was announced I hadn't been expecting it so it took Bondie digging me in the ribs for me to realise that they'd said my name. He's stronger than he thinks. I was rubbing my ribs for weeks after that.

I think he'd been on something; weed, blow, or some such. He was always more rock 'n' roll than me. It hadn't been an issue until that night, when he'd insisted on joining me on the stage. He could play the drums and had never received an award so I thought, "What's the harm?"

If only he'd stuck to the rules; walked up the aisle, to the podium, said 'thank you' to the celebrity who hands you the statue (in our case it was the teen pop sensation Jenson Penn) but Bondie's brain couldn't compute that. I don't think it computes anything these days.

He had to go up there didn't he and dig, dig, dig. Okay, so we're not a fan of the weak pop music that climbs the charts faster than we ever did in our heyday, but he's still sore that Jenson beat us to the top of the album chart when we released our Greatest Hits.

A term I use loosely as the record company in their limited wisdom to make it a double CD when we'd only had half a dozen 'hits' (top forty) so the rest were more fillers than a tub of sandwich spread. That's one thing I hadn't noticed; that he'd not been eating, Bondie, only drinking, picking at his food, fork never reaching his mouth, although it's big enough.

So there I was, mouth open to say a few unrehearsed words and ended up goldfish-like while Bondie spouted.

Bondie's real name's James… Bond, but he hates that. His mum was a real fan and we all reckon that she married a Bond just so she could have a son with the right name. Had the boy straight away, stroke of luck really, then the two of them left when he was still young. Probably why he is the way he is. Needed a father figure to straighten him out.

Anyway. He'd said his bit and I thought we were going to leave… he'd said plenty for both of us, what was I going to do, apologise? Pretend it didn't happen?

But then Jenson called him by his real name, don't know how he knew, Wikipedia I suppose, and well, Bondie flipped and went for the jugular, Jenson's jugular. Did enough so the damage was done.

Only temporary, thankfully, but he had to cancel his tour. Bondie received so many "thank you" letters after we could have wallpapered our bus… the one we toured on not long after the awards ceremony.

## RIP Lenny 'Shades' Froug

Characters as colourful as Lenny 'Shades' Froug don't come along very often and the world is most certainly a darker place without him.

Born Leonard Dennis Froug on the fourth of May 1943, the only son to Dennis Froug Snr and Lila Froug neé Smith, of Northamptonshire, England, Lenny ignored fashion trends, wearing stripes with spots, snakeskin with floral, and neon with nylon. He earned his nickname not by the sunglasses he wore – he loved direct contact with the sun – but by those worn by the people around him on his particularly colourful days.

As soon as he could talk, Leonard Jnr told his parents that he only had a limited time to live and wanted to fill it with as many experiences as he could. Being an only child, he was not short of love and attention, forming the easy-going personality that endeared him to everyone he met.

As a child, he would venture into his father's shed, help with Dennis Snr's experiments and soon he was trying his own, with success, leading him to ultimately find the cure to the common cold, all strains of cancer known to man, and some unknown, and why the underneath of a yoghurt pot lid always falls the wrong side down (gravital proportion to the square coverage of surface area on each side).

With those achievements, all before the age of twelve, under one's belt – in his case, a skinny rattlesnake – some would then have taken a step back and settle into a more normal life, but Lenny would regularly be spotted jetting off to war-torn countries where he would take over the peace negotiations and bring them to a satisfactory conclusion – the Gaza Strip now a nature reserve, to parched and famished African countries where he would dance his version of a rain dance, powerful enough to whip up the fiercest of rainstorms, filling the Froug Developments' wells deep enough to last the rest of the century.

One of many figments of English writer, Morgen Bailey's imagination, who herself is famous for killing off many of her characters, she and Leonard had a short (five hundred and forty-six-word), but endearing relationship and Ms Bailey is quoted as saying, "I wish I could have known Lenny better. Maybe I'll bring him back to life in a later story."

Those who knew Lenny, are devastated by his early demise and are, at the time of this item going to press, raising funds for his return.

Lenny leaves behind his parents, Dennis and Lila, and a hamster called 'Pixie'.

The memorial service will be held on fourteenth May at the Chapel in the grounds of the Leonard Froug Garden on Mars's Fourth Quadrant, near to the florescent rock pools that Lenny loved so much.

A free shuttle bus will be available from all UK airports, where Lenny was a season ticket holder, and Mr and Mrs Froug welcome attendees back to their home, Froug Mansions, which Lenny bought them with the money he received from his seventeenth Nobel Prize.

Those attending are forbidden from wearing black, including underwear – security guards have been instructed to check – and a disco will be held after the service in stretch marquees in the grounds of his home – formerly known as Buckingham Palace – until 'late'.

## Standing Room Only

With the only space on the bus next to you, standing room only, this is the opportunity you've been waiting for, to say "hello". You've smiled at each other for weeks, but not one word. You don't know his name – no one knows each other's names on the number forty-two. He shows his pass to the driver, who you think is called Hawk but his badge just says 'driver', as if he could be anything else.

It was the same on the train, a core of familiar faces for six years, grey suits amongst black ones, Financial Times mingling with Daily Mails and Kindles, but you want this to be different.

And now he's standing next to you, rain soaked, with his hair sticking to his head. There's a stray hair you want to move away from his eyes, the eyes that pull you in every time they meet yours. He reminds you of Mr Darcy and you wish he'd take off his jacket so you could see how damp his shirt is.

He smiles then looks down at his shoes. You look too, knowing they'll be one of three pairs, all black, just different stitching, all polished as if they're going to be inspected at any moment, and they now are… by him.

He coughs and looks up. "Not good for the leather," he says and you nod.

"Kills suede too," you say, never imagining that those would be the first words you say to him. You wanted them to be more romantic, invite him for a coffee, lunch perhaps or a film, but you know big talk starts with small talk, and even the weather as a topic thrills you.

What you say next will be pivotal, you want to take your time but a woman rings the bell, moves towards the front of the bus and he's looking at her empty seat, so you have to be quick.

You go to speak but he says, "There's a seat there if you'd like it."

"I'm fine, but thanks," you reply and grip tighter on to the handrail as the bus lurches round a bend.

"Me too," he says, and another standing passenger takes advantage, thumping down and stuffing his case between his calves.

There are only a couple of stops until you have to leave and you're debating whether to stay on, be late for work, take the day off even, when you spot the white cable running from his right ear. "What are you listening to?"

"Classical. A bit of everything but Erik Satie at the moment."

"Gnossienne or Gymnopédies?"

He laughs. "You know your Satie."

"My favourite, next to Beethoven."

"Much underrated."

"Satie?"

He nods. "You get off at St Giles, don't you."

"At the top, yes."

"Nice part of town."

"Not too noisy." You cringe as the small talk shrinks further.

"What do you do?" he asks, as if he read your mind.

"Lawyer. Property. Pretty dull really."

"Why dull?"

"Office-based. Little action."

"You'd rather have your day in court?"

You laugh. "Something like that."

Your stop approaches and you know staying on isn't an option. "This is me."

"It is," he replies, then holds out his hand. "Tom Shaw. See you tomorrow."

You shake his hand and smile. "Austin Kennedy. 'Til then."

## Sentimental Keepsake

It was the little girl in the red jacket that Eileen remembered the most from Schindler's List.

She'd imagined it was her mother, she'd have been about the right age. Hilda had a prominent nose but that was the only similarity. She didn't speak German, never had an interest in going there, and certainly wouldn't watch any war movies, favouring comedies, and the lightest of family dramas.

"Life is hard enough than to be reminded of it," she'd say.

Eileen knew her mother had had her ups and downs but couldn't imagine anything would have been as bad as that, but understood living that era had been close enough, so didn't press the matter.

It was too late to ask. Eileen wished she could turn the clock back a few months, to when they had their long conversations every other month when Eileen visited from her Scottish home. She should have persevered with the idea of Hilda writing her autobiography, recall those missing years hushed into the corners of her mind. Like an old house, the dust was swept aside, different memories uncovered during each visit.

It was only in the last few months of her mother's life that Eileen started to write things down, the last few weeks recorded on her Dictaphone. She would recount previous conversations, to check her facts, only to be met by blank stares as if the events had happened to someone else. Even mention of Iain, who Eileen had been too young to remember, would merit a tilt of the head and the offer of another cup of tea.

Then a few weeks later, Eileen had received the call she'd been dreading, travelled the journey long enough to dictate earlier conversations and the jobs ahead.

There followed the paperwork, the funeral, distant relatives giving their condolences to a woman they barely knew. Eileen had put her mother's house on the market and set to the task of dividing her possessions between charity shop, skip and sentimental keepsakes.

In one of the drawers in the bedroom's dresser, Eileen found an envelope containing a small silver key, with it a note of the bank and box number. Having lived frugal lives, it was the last thing Eileen had expected so she drove straight there and asked to see the box.

She'd taken her mother's death certificate and probate documentation and after a phone call and hushed conversation, the bank manager had introduced Eileen to his colleague who would show her the vault.

The man shut the door behind him, leaving Eileen alone surrounded by what felt like her school's changing room, only the lockers would have held much richer contents.

Eileen stared at the metal box labelled '147', and turned over the key in her hand. Like the room, it felt alien. Her box was one of the biggest and yet, she guessed, one of the lightest; not light enough to be empty but not containing weighty jewels, bonds or cash that she suspected the others housed.

The key glided into its hole and turned easily. Lifting the lid slowly, it made no noise but as Eileen let it fall open, she leapt back as it clanked onto the hard counter top and exposed the contents within. Just one item: a child's red woollen jacket.

## Ghost

As you rattle the charity tin, you sense something non-metal; a button you reckon.

Then a man walks up to you with a coloured piece of paper in his hand, an off-red you think, but it's small so you can't quite see. He folds it into a sliver, small enough for the slot on the top of your tin. He does it slowly, not to show off but out of reverence, but it lets you see what it is. A fifty pound note. He doesn't particularly look as if he can afford it but he gives it as if it recompenses for something he's earned, something non-monetary, something sacred.

"Thank you," you beam, hoping to catch his glance which is still staring at the tin. It reminds you of the scene from Ghost where Whoopi Goldberg unwillingly gives some nuns a huge cheque, only this chap isn't unwilling, just deep in thought.

You look either side of him and smile in case there's a female Patrick Swayze encouraging him to part with his hard-earned money.

The man just nods, turns and leaves, and you imagine his 'ghost' walking beside him, telling him he's done the right thing, that the money is better off in there, the exact words you're failing to recall. Only this isn't four million dollars. But, you guess, to some it may as well be. To those it's going to, that's exactly what it is.

The tin's getting full so you walk to your fellow volunteer, Angie, a few shops down, and tell her you're going to pop back to HQ for an empty tin. It's a five-minute drive so you know she won't be alone for long.

As you pull up, you spot Jay, one of the paid members of staff, walking into the building. You catch up with him as he heads for the office and swap "hello"s.

He puts his container on the desk and empties it out. You watch the coins roll into a controlled heap and a couple of notes flutter; a blue five, a brown ten. You're not one to score points but you know you've done better.

Holding out your container, you ask, "Can I swap this for an empty one please?"

"I'm sorry, they're all out," he says. "You could have mine but I'm heading back. Won't take me a second to empty yours though."

"Sure," you say and watch him cut the cable ties holding the lid in place. He smiles as your coins pile out next to his, and they remind you of the Henry Mountains that one time you visited the States.

"Oh look," he says, pulling at the fifty-pound note. "It's a cheque."

"Really?" you say as he unfolds it. "I could have sworn…"

"Oh!"

Your heart sinks and imagine it being for a fiver instead of fifty pounds. "Oh, well…"

"No, you don't understand. It's a cheque for…"

"Yes?" you say, hoping for a figure near the fifty.

"Two million, four hundred and seventy-five thousand pounds."

"Please don't exaggerate, Jay," you say but he smiles and holds out his hand.

What you thought was a fifty-pound note really is a cheque. A very pretty off-red cheque from The Patrick Swayne Foundation. Not Swayze but Swayne. Just a coincidence. The cheque however, doing a quick calculation in your head, isn't. It's worth about four million dollars.

## Two Short

Karen felt as if she'd been living in a bubble all these years… twenty-three. Two short of their silver anniversary and too short is what she'd turned out to be.

Before she'd had a chance to give him his card, bring out the voucher from her handbag, tell him she'd booked their favourite restaurant for lunch, Emrys had announced at breakfast that he'd met someone else.

He told Karen off for being emotional when she'd asked who the woman was. "No one you know," he'd answered, but he'd never been a good liar.

"It's Eloise… isn't it?" Karen had stuttered, tears streaming down her face.

He'd gone quiet, eyes down at the newspaper she knew he was only half reading.

Eloise, his PA, had been the obvious choice, they spent so much time together. She was the female version of him; thin and all legs.

Karen stood opposite him at the dining room table, hands gripping the back of one of the chairs, her knuckles turning white as it became clear that he was enjoying the discussion.

She wanted to ask him how long it had been going on, how serious it was, what was going to happen now but instead she watched him slurp his tea, wipe his nose on his sleeve, and laugh like a machine gun at something in the paper.

"Okay, bye," she said and walked into lounge, turned on the TV and changed the channel to one she wanted to watch. She listened to him drag back his chair, dump his breakfast dishes into the sink and plod upstairs.

Moments later, he thumped a suitcase back down the stairs and pulled up its handle as he reached the hall. Putting on his jacket as he walked into the lounge, he coughed, but Karen ignored him.

He coughed again.

She hit the mute button and looked up. "Yes?"

"I'm off."

"Like bad wine," she said and smiled, surprised at herself.

"Don't be like that."

"I can be however I like. I'm single now." Then it hit her, she was, she could do whatever she wanted for the first time in more than half her lifetime. She tapped the mute button again and the voices sprang back into action.

As she listened to Emrys wheel his case, haul it over the threshold and slam the front door, she reached into her bag, pulled out the voucher and stared at it.

She wanted to tear it into little pieces, tear Emrys into little pieces, but she'd never recoup the money she'd spent on it, so she dialled the number on the back.

Before she could ask whether it was transferrable or refundable, she'd made an appointment for the following morning.

After the best night's sleep she'd had in years, she showered, dressed and ate a small breakfast.

Grabbing her handbag, car keys and jacket, she left the house, closing the front door gently, tenderly stroking the red-painted wood as if it now belonged only to her.

Driving along the dual carriageway, she put her foot down pretending she was Stirling Moss or Lewis Hamilton, until she reached her exit. Following the signs, she pulled into the visitor's car park.

With the voucher in her hand, she strode towards the reception and past the sign saying, 'Welcome to Silverstone'.

## All-Inclusive Package

I flinched as the cell door slammed. You'd think it would be worst the first night but then I still had hope.

It'll be a month on Friday and they're still wrangling, 'them' being the British Embassy and Thai authorities.

There's no doubt about Flynn, but we're being tried together and I'm a grey area.

Carrier. Mule. Whatever you want to call me. 'Wife' is what Flynn calls… called me. Wife of thirty-seven days. The dream holiday, all-inclusive package: wedding, honeymoon – romantic ceremony for four… five if you include the celebrant, our hotel manager. They're multi-talented over here.

Too, as it turns out, is Flynn; liar, con artist, thief. Not sure if he's a cheat yet but it doesn't matter anymore. We'll see each other in court and that'll be that.

The lawyer they've given me says I could get ten years. Ten years! For carrying my suitcases, but not checking them properly.

Did I pack them myself? Of course you're going to say "yes", even if you didn't, which I did. Thought I had. Had.

Did I, at any time, leave them unattended? You're going to say, "no". Of course I hadn't left them alone, not since we'd left the hotel. The taxi driver loaded everything into his boot and I sat beside him all the way, nearly an hour.

I get travel-sick so Flynn let me sit in the front. He's… he was good like that. We didn't stop once so no way anyone could have interfered with them.

Then we went straight from the taxi to check-in. That went okay, as did the x-ray but I knew it would because we had nothing new in our hand luggage, all our souvenirs were in our cases.

The security check was okay. They lingered over Flynn's passport but let us through. You always feel guilty even when there's no need. We were fine on the trip out so there was no reason not to be on the return.

My lawyer's due back today. Don't know when but…

It's just how you imagine it to be here, how you might have seen it on TV. I'm lucky. I have a corner to myself, and a seat. Some have to stand. We all have our spaces, like a book club meeting. Someone goes and you get to take their place, try to get a place before it's offered to you and they don't let you forget it.

We've just hit fifty in here. I count every time I wake up but it only ever changes in the day. No one comes at night. The women are mostly around my age, mid to late thirties. We only get one shower a day and clean clothes once a week so it's not nice but we're all in the same… boat.

At least we had our holiday. Could have been caught arriving but then as far as I know Flynn bought the stuff here, or was given it. I don't know.

They interviewed… interrogated us in separate rooms, told me all about him, who he really is. His name's the same, before you think that he's that kind of con man, but all the other things he's done… I'm just one of a long line, at the end of it, I guess, but when you're in love…

Hello? Yes. Yes, that's me.

## Weapon of Choice

The red scarf, he'd decided would be his weapon of choice. Ironic, given that it was her favourite.

He'd plotted this moment all day; romantic dinner, superb wine, get her in the 'mood' then he'd do it.

She loved him saying what he was going to do to her – gave her something to look forward to – only there were some things she didn't need to know. Telling her he'd kiss her neck was fine, but saying he was going to wrap it in red silk and squeeze it until she stopped breathing would only spoil the moment for them both.

He'd kiss then caress her neck, let her feel the scarf soft against her skin, stand behind her, a position of strength. She'd struggle of course, try to scratch his hands but she bit her nails so they'd have little effect. Besides, he was a foot taller, heavier.

As he walked up the path to the cottage, a bottle of Mas de Daumas Gassac in one hand, the other inside his right jacket pocket, she opened the door and smiled. He followed her inside, right hand feeling the soft material that had lain there all day, since he'd removed it from her dressing table that morning.

They went into the kitchen where she'd already started cooking, the smell of his favourite meal, beef goulash, permeating the air.

"I've got something to tell you," she said, but he knew what she was going to say; that she'd found someone else, that she didn't want to be with him anymore, that this was the last meal they'd share together. He'd known for weeks, could tell she was 'acting', that something wasn't right.

Placing the wine bottle on the kitchen table, he went over to the stove and stood behind her as she stirred the goulash, then watched her lean over to smell the sauce. Although he was hungry, he'd hardly touched breakfast, skipped lunch, the thought of sharing a meal with her now made him feel sick.

There'd be no last meal, no small talk, no "I'm sorry" conversation.

Pulling out the scarf, he wrapped each end round his wrists and pulled it tight, then brought it over her head and in front of her neck. He saw her head lower, her gaze following the scarf.

"Oh, that's where it went," she said and laughed, a laugh he used to find endearing but had more recently found annoying, like a schoolgirl's, immature, almost babyish. She stopped laughing as he brought the two ends behind her neck and crossed them tightly. "Ow," she said, putting her free hand up to her neck, "lighten up a little, will you, darling."

But he didn't lighten up, he squeezed, his biceps pressing against his pale blue work shirt.

He heard the clank of the spoon as she dropped it into the saucepan and pulled at the scarf, her fingers clawing at his, her voice no longer understandable but a rasp that faded as she slumped to the floor.

That's when he saw the envelope, on the work surface, her name in writing he didn't recognise and he knew he'd done the right thing. He stepped over her body, lunged at the envelope and tugged out the single sheet of paper.

As the photograph revealed itself, he saw the scan, the human peanut surrounded by a black and white blur. He screamed as it fell to the ground.

## What He Saw

*Red sky at night, shepherd's delight,*

*Red sky in morning, fisherman's warning.*

I had a dream. That's what Martin Luther King said, wasn't it? Oh no, present tense, "have a dream".

I had one too, the other night, except it wasn't half as nice as his. I was stuck in traffic… on a motorway, I think it was. Stationary, in the fast lane, silver barriers dented and bruised. I remember there was a lorry in the lane to my left. Never liked lorries much… big cumbersome things, but we have to have food, don't we.

So there I was, waiting for some kind of life from the cars in front, when it got dark. I looked out my side window expecting to see rain but the sky was cloudless. Bluer than I'd seen in a while too, or maybe it was just because I was paying attention for once. No, I do pay attention. I'm a painter so I take note. Up here, the old brain cells.

Anyway, with nothing happening in that direction, I looked back ahead and that's when I saw it, the lorry… tipping over… to its right, with me in its middle. Of course I couldn't go forwards, car blocking my way, so I swung round to look over my left shoulder, through my car, to see if I could reverse.

Stupid. Of course I couldn't, I was in a traffic jam. What I should have done was to get out, run like hell, but in dreams you don't think of things like that, do you. You have no control.

You could be screaming at yourself but it would make no difference, you do what your sub-sub-conscious does, not your sub-conscious. Two layers of you like a sponge cake. I had to laugh when I thought of that, what with the red raspberry jam they usually use. No, I know, not tasteful. Sorry about that.

It shook me up. Still had it in my brain when I left the house. Not sure why because I don't even have a car.

Wasn't really awake anyway, being that early, but had to catch the light. Brody was a sport too but he said he didn't mind, that he was often up at that time to go fishing.

I'd picked the perfect spot, just off the main road, by the fence over the river, beautiful even without the sky. I reckon he thinks I'm a bit mad, that it would be too ordinary when there are plenty of other things to paint. But I wanted to paint him, he's quirky-looking, since he lost his hair.

And he was there already, in that long navy top he's addicted to. His wife must be sick of washing it.

I settled on him standing near the end of the bridge so I could get the river in, a nice swirl of blue, trailing off behind him, the banks either side. I set up my easel and was about to start when I spotted a couple, walking, in the distance. At first I wasn't best pleased but then thought, *Hey, why not*.

Then I spotted Brody's expression, wide-eyed like he was trying to stretch the sleep out of his eyes. The easel slipped a little, so I grabbed it, instinct, losing my focus on Brody. Sound without the vision. The sound of him calling my name, "Edvard! Edvard" before I could look up or turn round.

## Charity Shops On Saturday

As the front door opened, Tracey and Dawn stared at each other. No words were spoken but each knew what the other was thinking as a man and his four teenage children trudged through the shop with two large black sacks each, depositing them in the back room.

The two ladies smiled and nodded at the donors as they trawled back out, like worker ants going about their day.

Noon on a late spring Saturday, a bright and sunny Saturday lunchtime following a very wet week. Nothing special in that, you might think, but wet weather keeps people indoors, so plenty of time to purge, to spring clean.

The onslaught of donations had started even before the shop had opened. Tracey had arrived first, unable to get to the front door because of the mound of black sacks… damp wet sacks from being out in the rain all night.

One had been torn open – Tracey guessed by bargain hunters – with the contents sprawled out towards the pedestrian crossing, the pedestrians from which were walking through the clothes rather than stepping over, or heaven forbid, picking them up and putting them with the bags from which they had been excreted.

The steady flow of donations throughout that morning turned into a flood as the local car boot sales finished, the shop an easy drop-off point on the way home. Just peeling the white price stickers off the bric-a-brac would be a job designated to one of the two volunteers due in that afternoon.

Charity shops rely on their volunteers… They have piped audio that tells us this and like most shops they never have enough, so when the lady who'd held the door open (without thanks) for the man and his children, came to the counter to buy three blouses and a pair of trousers but more importantly, to ask for a volunteer form, Dawn and Tracey were thrilled.

They'd seen her before, a semi-regular customer, always polite, often laden with purchases and always paying cash so the shop would be charged no commission on whatever plastic card she might have used.

Unlike some (which had resulted in a sign behind the counter), she didn't haggle over the prices, she always brought her own bag and never paid for a fifty pence item with a twenty-pound note. She was the ideal customer and now she wanted to work with them… for free.

Dawn and Tracey were used to handing out volunteer forms and never seeing them, or the requestee again, but they lived in hope this time, knowing the lady's track record.

As Dawn handed her the form, the lady looked at it, squinted and frowned.

Again, Tracey and Dawn stared at each other with their telepathic code. Before either of them could speak, the lady put the form onto the counter, saying, "Oh dear."

"Is there a problem?" Dawn asked gently.

The lady nodded.

"Something we can help you with?" Tracey chipped in.

The lady nodded again. "I've forgotten my glasses."

"You don't have to fill it in now," Tracey continued but then wished she hadn't, given the history of other forms that had left the premises, never to return.

"Would you fill it in for me?" the lady asked.

"Of course," Dawn said, pen to hand, pulling the form nearer. "Date… the eighth… shop, Okay… Can I have your name please?"

"Certainly," the lady said with a broad beam. "Gibbs… Charity Gibbs."

## Treacle Tart

That last slice of treacle tart has my name on it. I know it runs the risk of me not getting my silver star at class Monday night but I deserve it. Been good all week, I have, so a little splurge won't hurt. It's only Friday, I can be good at the weekend. Besides, it's only a little piece… by comparison to the whole thing.

Bit of a queue but they're all suits, they'll go for sandwiches or the meal deal; sarnie, crisps and a drink, low calorie usually, they look the type. You know, a swim before work, weights or treadmill on the way home.

I never had a problem with my weight until I met Declan, then meals out, cooking for two, it just piled on. Ironic then that he left me for our next-door neighbour, so skinny she'd disappear behind a lamppost. I guess that's what he likes to do. Meet someone, fatten them up then move on.

So then I started comfort eating and here – Butler's Bakery – became my second home until I ran out of clothes and couldn't afford to buy any more, so signed up with Belly Busters.

Two weeks, six pounds. Another pound and I get a silver star. Seven more after that and I get a gold one. I'll have more stars than that Hollywood pavement… sidewalks they call them, don't they.

You know, where they get them to kneel down and get their hands all dirty. Show's they're human, that they don't mind doing that.

It's having everything still warm that's the clincher, from Butler's. More expensive than the supermarket, granted, but most of the supermarket's stuff's been there since yesterday. I know because one of the doughnut's still has my thumbprint in it. And it's why it has no queue either.

My favourite's the Chelsea Bun – peel layers off as I walk home. I used to buy two, or more, so there'd be something left to look forward to. Someone's beaten me to them today, so it's treacle tart. Find them a bit sweet, if I'm honest.

Great, nearly there. One, two… fourth. That's okay. At the front, there's Earl the builder (loves bending over as the girls go by and they always giggle) – English breakfast in a bap – then Old Mrs Tomlinson – seeded batch and scotch egg. I'm good with people. Working in a hairdressers for so many years, you get to find out a lot about the human race.

Don't know the lady in front of me. Nice perfume; sweet but not overpowering. Meal deal for sure.

Earl. Breakfast in a bap, check. And Coke and a Kit Kat.

Mrs T. Seeded batch and two scotch eggs! Pushing the boat out today.

Okay. Perfume lady. Ham salad sandwich. Cheese? Okay. Diet Coke. Of course… Crisps now. Ready salted, I think. It's not difficult, dear. They've only got a choice of three.

No, don't point over there. Phew. Yes, the Eccles do look nice. No. Changed your mind again. No wonder they have a queue. The assistant should be firmer. Give us all a time slot.

Of course I always know what I want before I get to the counter. The displays are clear enough to choose before…

No! Go back to the Eccles. No! Not the… please don't. What am I going to have if you go for the…?

Bye, treacle tart. And you look so good…

## Wait, Listen, And Wait Some More

It wasn't another planet but it might as well have been. Bradford. Why had he brought me to Bradford?

Nostalgia, he'd said, but I didn't know anyone there. Here. It's full of… well, Yorkshire people with funny accents and a 'pudding' you eat with beef. The only puddings I know of are the type you eat with ice cream, or cream if you're lucky.

A new start, he told me.

He? Oh, yeah, that's Drake, my son. Married to Cara. Barely married at that. That's why they needed a new start.

I told them they should have left me down south. Three is most certainly not company, or is it two? I forget.

Oh yes, Bradford. Drake insisted we'd been before. Lots of times, he'd said but nothing looked familiar. Too modern for me, and what was I supposed to do? Drake had his new job and… Cara. Should remember that, they've been together long enough.

How many years? They had a party recently, before we moved. Silly timing. There were boxes everywhere but Drake said it would double-up as a leaving do. I don't think he really wanted to go but Cara wasn't too happy and she's a northerner so she got her way.

She's not found a job yet but then she'll be busy settling us all in.

I've got a lovely room right at the top of the house. I was worried about the stairs but they said they'll get one of those Stanley chairs. No, not Stanley. Air. Air line. Stanline. Something like that.

Cara's organising it. She's good like that. Was a secretary. Can't understand why she can't get a job. Drake's a doctor so she could work for him but he says she's worked for international companies so I guess she wants something a bit more… you know, grand.

So they've put me up here and I have to wait for the electric stair chair. It'll be fun; pressing buttons. It's even got a joy stick, Drake said. I thought he was being rude until he showed me the picture.

I could even have different coloured cushions so I went for something with flowers, pansies I think, so it would feel like I'm going out in the garden, although I'll be sitting on it so I won't see it, which is a shame.

It's the garden I'll miss most. Can't understand why they'd choose somewhere so big that had a yard for a garden, all concrete and plant pots. Used to spend hours pottering, I did. Now I'll have to potter around the house, make sure I don't get in Cara's way. Not that I can up here.

I hear her singing to the radio sometimes. I've asked for one of my own. Mine was in the box of things that went missing when we moved. Had to be mine, didn't it. Had all my photos of Maurice in it. All but one. Still have the locket round my neck. Not taken it off in fifty years.

He was a handsome man, my Maurice. Wouldn't mind being stuck up here if I had him to keep me company, but I can't complain. Cara makes me nice meals; breakfast, lunch.

After that of course she's busy getting everything ready for when Drake comes home. He can't expect her to be up here with me when he's been away from her all day. So I wait, listen, and wait some more.

## The One She'd Bought The Dress For

As the hand clasped around her waist, Jade wriggled in vain to escape.

The music slowed, the lights dimmed, and Jade smiled politely at Mackenzie Felsham, the school nerd, who twenty years on, looked little different; glasses as thick as double-glazing, cress from the hours-old triangular sandwiches poking out from between his tobacco-stained teeth. He was the last person Jade wanted to slow dance with but his sad expression made it hard for her to leave.

"No name badge," Mackenzie said.

"No, it wouldn't stick."

"Doesn't matter, I'd remember you anywhere, Jade Allen. Nice dress by the way," he said, smiling broadly.

Jade kept her gaze on his eyes to avoid his mouth. "Thanks. It's new."

"Suits you," Mackenzie said, pulling her even closer.

The three or four minutes of 'Three Times a Lady' was ruined by Mackenzie singing loudly, and out of tune. Everyone else had stopped dancing to stare at Jade.

Before she could say she had to go, the music changed, the lights went up. Mackenzie pushed her away before pulling her back in again, curling her into his chest.

Thrusting out his right hand, he led Jade into a tango and strutted across the room.

As Jade sped past her old classmates, she spotted the one she'd wanted to see, the only one she'd missed, the one she'd bought the dress for… Rafe Harper, all six feet four of him, still with the sportsman physique and all-year tan.

He smiled at her and nodded.

As she mouthed a "help!", he shook his head, the smile turning into a laugh, but then stood in their way, forcing Mackenzie to stop.

"May I cut in?" Rafe asked him.

Mackenzie frowned. "Well…"

"It's only fair," Jade piped up.

"Very well," Mackenzie conceded.

As Rafe took Mackenzie's place and Jade's hands in his, she noticed his wedding ring. "You're married!" she said before she could help herself.

Rafe looked at the wide platinum band then over to the corner of the room. "Yeah, Michelle's in the toilet. Nice dress, by the way."

"Thank you, it's new," Jade said with as little enthusiasm as she'd shown Mackenzie.

As she and Rafe danced, Jade looked towards the toilets waiting for his wife to appear.

Just as the song was ending, a stunning brunette appeared and Jade's heart sank further. She was as beautiful as Jade had expected but she'd seen her before, in the dress shop, the assistant who'd shown her the dress, said how much it suited her.

Jade hadn't been sure until Mackenzie had complimented her and then when Rafe had said the same, she'd known it was the right choice, until Michelle had appeared… wearing exactly the same dress, except a couple of sizes smaller.

Jade and Rafe stopped dancing and as Michelle crossed the room, Jade noticed behind her a tall dark-haired man also walking towards them. Jade stood up a little straighter, put her shoulders back and smiled. *Keep coming*, she thought, *don't stop, don't veer off, be single*. He didn't look like anyone she'd gone to school with, a year above perhaps.

The woman waved at someone Jade didn't recognise and walked off to the side of the room.

Jade turned to Rafe who was still looking ahead and smiling. She turned back and only saw the man, then it all fell into place.

"Hi, darling," Rafe said as the man reached them. "Michel," Rafe said in a French accent, "J'aimerais te présenter…" Rafe turned back to Jade. "Sorry, what was your name?"

## Same Time Tomorrow

Wayne looked at the woman as he approached the bench. She was beautiful, and beyond the reach of someone like him, but where better to be while eating his sandwiches. “Do you mind if I sit?”

“Not at all,” she said, smiling. “I’ll budge up.” She was so slim that she took up hardly any space on the old wooden bench, but had the largest handbag he’d ever seen. A bag she’d hauled onto the floor to make room for him.

“That’s sweet,” he said, pointing to the bench.

“Not a problem,” she replied.

“No, I meant the plaque.”

The woman looked over her shoulder. “Oh yes. In memory of Santiago Denby. Beloved father of Truman, grandfather to Rufus. No women.”

“Sorry?”

“Three generations of men but no women.”

“Oh.”

“You wanted to sit?”

“Yes, thank you.” He sat down and took out a sandwich.

“Why do you think there are no women?” the woman continued.

“Perhaps they just weren’t around?

“The grandchild being male is fair enough but no grandmother, no mother.”

“Maybe they’re dead too, something hereditary perhaps… you know, before Santiago Denby.”

“That’s too sad.”

“Not enough room on the plaque?”

“They could have had a bigger one.”

“I guess, although it’s a small bench.” Wayne patted the bench’s arm.

“True but…”

“Maybe the three of them had a special bond?”

“Like a boys club.”

Wayne nodded. “Exactly.”

“That would be nice.”

"Maybe there's another bench with the women on."

The woman smiled. "Not in this park, I've sat on them all."

"All? How many are there?"

The woman tucked a strand of hair behind her ear. "Eleven… including this one."

"With inscriptions?"

"No. Only three… well, four; this one's new. I usually sit nearer the lake but…"

"But?"

"It's silly really."

"Go on."

"The schools are off and there are loads of people feeding the ducks."

"You don't like ducks?"

She shrugged. "They're okay. It's the geese really. They can be nasty."

"It would be the children for me," Wayne said without thinking.

The woman threw back her head and laughed. Her teeth were immaculate and Wayne bit on his lip as he suddenly became conscious of his tobacco-stained ones.

"Do you have children?" Wayne asked, hoping he'd not put his foot in it.

"God, no," she replied. "I had a narrow escape once."

Wayne waited, hoping she'd elaborate but she changed the subject.

"What are your sandwiches?"

"Coronation Chicken."

"My favourite."

Wayne pointed to them. "I have two if you'd like…?"

"No, you're fine. I've eaten, but thank you."

"What did you have?" Wayne asked, then blushed as he realised how small their small talk had become.

"Cheese wrap, more boring than it sounds but it's all I had in the fridge that was still edible."

"Been away?"

"Bali."

"Wow."

"Again very boring."

"It's always looked lovely on the TV."

"It is but not when you only see it from an aeroplane."

The woman seeing Wayne's puzzled expression added, "Air stewardess. The occasional stop-over but even then it's all shop talk, and after twenty years, it gets a bit…"

Wayne didn't think she looked old enough to have working that long but was relieved that made them a similar age.

She held out a hand. "Rebecca."

"Wayne," he said, and blushed again.

"Lovely to meet you, Wayne. I should go actually, sorry," she said. "Nothing in the house. Same time tomorrow?"

Wayne nodded. "Look forward to it," he said and watched her leave before finishing his sandwich and heading to the chemist to buy some stain-removing toothpaste and nicotine gum.

## The Photographer That No One Else Can Get

"She told me she loved me."

"Diana?"

The old man nodded.

The journalism student noted it down. "When was that?"

"August fourth 1997, my birthday."

"But that's…"

"I know. Not long before…"

"Where were you?"

"Paris. She came here a lot."

"With Dodi?"

The old man nodded again. "She said she was going to leave him but…"

"Go on."

"She couldn't."

"Why couldn't she?"

"I can't tell you, I promised."

"It won't do anyone any harm now, not after all these years."

"She has family. Grandchildren… great grandchildren soon. No, it'll never come out."

"But you're telling me now."

"You won't believe me and you won't say anything, or print it. It's too big a risk from an old fool."

"I do believe you, Mr…"

"James. Call me James."

"But I… oh. I'm Naomi. I do believe you, Mr James, that's why I'm here."

"Not Mr, just James. Then you'll know about the photographs, and the car."

"Car?"

"My old white Fiat. Long gone. A square cube of metal used as someone's coffee table, no doubt."

"So there *was* a Fiat."

"I read about it in the papers of course, so someone must have seen me but nothing ever happened. I waited, hid the car in a deserted barn until I knew the coast was clear then gave it to a scrap dealer on the condition he'd strip it for parts then crush it. He was a friend of a friend so I believed him. Never heard anything so…"

"And you have photographs?"

"Of course. Loads. Not printed, couldn't have evidence lying around, so I left them on the disk. The non-floppy floppy kind."

Naomi smiled as James continued.

"I didn't need to print them anyway, or ever look at them again. I have them all… up here," he said, tapping his forehead.

"Where is it now, the disk?"

"In the car."

Staring out to the car park, Naomi asked, "You still drive?"

The old man laughed. "No! Don't be silly, dear. I'm knocking on a hundred. In the Fiat. The stick never came to light either so it's probably underneath someone's News of the World or remote control."

"They don't make the News of…" Naomi looked up when the manager, a tall plump woman with a red face, blocked the light from the window.

"Sorry folks, but it's meal time."

Naomi was about to ask another question, expecting to have a few minutes' grace, when the manager coughed overdramatically.

Closing her notebook, Naomi tucked it, along with her royal blue fountain pen, into her messenger bag. "Thank you, James. Do you mind if I come back another time?"

"Certainly, dear, but don't leave it too long. As I said, I'm knocking–"

"I'll see you out," the manager butted in, and the two women walked towards the building's exit.

"Get everything you wanted?"

"Almost."

"Which name did he give you?"

"James…"

"Ah, it's 007 is it today? Ms Windsor, we've had a stream of people here to see him over the years. Since he started saying… well, everything he's just told you. Don't believe a word of it. We let them in, let you in, to keep him amused, so I'm sorry that you've wasted your time but he just loves to make things up, bordering on cruel if you ask me, trying to make people believe his lies."

But of course the man wasn't lying. He just had a bad memory. He'd been going by different names all his life. Never knew what his real one was, having been left in a handbag in a cloakroom in Victoria Railway Station.

## Sally Never Listened

As holidays go, this was definitely going to be one of the most memorable.

Todd clicked on the right arrow, flicking through the array of photographs. The camera told him he was on number 173 of 1,729. The joy of digital. He was surprised there weren't more, although he had been through them, back in the hotel room, deleting the fuzzy ones. Following wildlife around on safari, there had been plenty of those.

He wished Sally had been there to see the results of the last few but then she would have said that 2D could never replace 3D, having a rhinoceros charge at you, a lion feeding its young, hyenas ripping apart… Todd didn't need to picture that image, he was looking at it.

He looked up as the announcement called for his flight. He picked up his bag and walked to Gate seventeen. This was the bit he usually loved and Sally usually hated but today he felt the same as she had. They were travelling on different flights and that felt too weird.

The woman in the blue and yellow uniform smiled as she took his boarding pass.

He tried to smile back but knew it was fake.

She read his name and her smile faded. She nodded and held out her arm to indicate his path.

He trudged in line, following the other passengers, some in suits, most in casual clothes. He was still in khaki, a last memory to his two-week vacation, one he didn't want to remember but knew he always would.

As the 'no seatbelt' sign dimmed, and as the man in the next seat asked to be let out, Todd removed his belt then swung his legs round. Todd watched the man walk up the aisle and into the toilet. His wife was staring out the window, hands gripping the seat arms.

Todd laughed, not just to himself, but out loud, to the whole plane, and he couldn't stop laughing.

As it became clear he was unnerving the other passengers, an air stewardess approached. "Is everything alright, sir?"

Todd nodded, tears rolling down his face.

"Is there anything I can do, sir?"

Todd shook his head, and wiped his cheek. "I told her…"

"Yes, sir?"

"I told her, my wife Sally, not to get too close but she wouldn't listen. She had to get out the jeep and see for herself. Had to get the best photographs. It was a new camera, you see. I bought it for her for our anniversary. She bought the holiday. Very brave, I thought, seeing as she doesn't… didn't like flying."

The stewardess looked at the woman staring out the window.

"Oh, that's not her," Todd said. "No, Sally's on the next flight."

The stewardess looked puzzled.

"They wouldn't let us travel together. I said I'd wait but–"

"That's terrible," the stewardess said half-heartedly, then went to attend to another passenger.

The woman carried on staring out the window as her husband returned. He took his seat and turned to Todd. "I hope you've not been trying to talk to her. You won't get anything unless you touch her. Deaf as a post. Never listens to a word I say. Still in shock, I suppose."

"Shock?"

"Oh yes, terrifying really. Came a bit too close to a pack of hyenas on one of our jaunts. They said afterwards that a woman did exactly the same thing the day before and wasn't so lucky. I'd told her to be careful but as I said, never listens to a word I say."

## One Out Of Three

Staring at the old school photo, it scares you how much Brandon looks like Addison.

Brandon's on a school trip today and you're missing him already. It's only been an hour but you know he'll not be giving you a moment's thought. His favourite place, the space museum. Typical boy, he loves anything big and shiny.

His teacher, Mrs Desmond, is your favourite. She's the woman you'd pick out for a grandmother if you had to, the times you wish your mother was still alive. She'd have told you what to do.

You feel like you're going wrong but you don't know how. You want to be better than Addison's new wife although you know she's no threat. She's too wrapped up in getting a family of her own to bother about the old one.

You're willing the post to come, the phone to ring, something with news of your interview. It felt like it went well but you're nervous all the same. It's nearby, school hours, and you know how much the extra money will help; Brandon can have new clothes and maybe after a while, you can buy a better car, not as big as Addison's but something that doesn't make you nervous every time you turn the key.

The radio's good on a Thursday and you keep yourself busy until it's time to collect your son. The post is only bills and the solitary call asks for the bridal shop so you tell them through gritted teeth to reverse the last two digits. They tell you how sorry they are but you just want them to hang up. There's 1571 but you don't want to miss the call.

Replaying the interview in your head as you drive, you realise Brandon's been talking, but you don't want to ask him to repeat, so say, "that's nice" and keep your eyes on the road. He's still talking when you get home and only pauses when you check the answerphone.

At dinner he tells you all about the machines that mean nothing to you, so you just smile as you serve up the shepherd's pie and gooseberry fool.

The next day brings no post or calls and they say no news is good news but you'd rather know, so you're still frustrated when Brandon brings home a photograph of his trip which you put on the mantelpiece for safekeeping. Saying it's nice, you mean to sound more genuine but he's already reading his Doctor Who comic and the moment's past.

Saturday morning, Brandon's waiting by the front door, ten minutes early. Addison's notoriously late and you want to tell Brandon not to get his hopes up, but then the doorbell rings and he pulls it open.

He throws his arms around his father's waist and is as swiftly encompassed. It's a sight you rarely see and you want to join them for a group hug but you know there's a boundary and it's 'their' time, so you back away quietly into the kitchen.

Leaving the door open so you can see through the crack, you watch Brandon drag his dad into the lounge and pull him to the mantelpiece. He removes the photograph and lifts it up.

You can't see him clearly but you swear Addison is crying.

"You look smashing, Brandon," he says, ruffling your son's hair, just like he used to do to his own whenever he'd had a shower. Remembering his physique, you smile then stop as you hear footsteps, and can't help blushing as Addison walks into the kitchen.

## Don't Talk To The Food

It was at times like this that Alex wished he wasn't human, that he didn't look odd, different to everyone else.

He knew they could change their shape, their form, be different colours, but he was just one, pink, and sometimes it got boring.

He was still trying to work out why he was there, what his purpose was. There had to be a purpose.

He'd watched the movies; the Hitchhiker's Guide to the Galaxy where there was someone like him, on a strange planet, The Wizard of Oz, Mork & Mindy, although Mork was an alien, he was someone who looked human, on earth, and this most definitely wasn't earth.

He'd moved a few times: from Cornwall to London, then London to Hull, Hull to Birmingham then Birmingham to Dorset. He knew all about cultures, each place was different. He only had to move a few miles and it felt odd. It would take a while to settle in, for the roads to become familiar.

What he wouldn't have given for a road, instead of the tram-like cars flying above his head. Everything vertical as well as horizontal.

This must be a tiny planet, he'd decided, he could see from one side to the other. There was little space to build around but boy, did they use every inch.

There were arguments, accidents, that part of this bizarre world was like earth. He was beginning to realise that regardless of the outside, the inside was pretty much the same. All feeling, arguing. Couldn't understand a word, of course.

The thing that struck him as most odd was that no one was taking any notice of him. There were lots of different creatures but they were all weird – they couldn't possibly think him weird, and therefore normal, could they?

He'd not been there long. He wasn't sure how long was, how the time went. It seemed to go the same sort of speed, it felt the same.

There was no sun, just a huge spotlight, made everything warm, not unpleasantly warm like underneath a takeaway heat lamp, but on a beach on a pleasant day – not quite so hot that you needed high-factor sun cream but that if you stay out in it too long you might burn. He'd always had fair skin.

He was trying to remember what had led him there, but he could only remember from when he'd awoken. It felt like the alien from Terminator one, Arnold Schwarzenegger as it turned out, only unlike Arnie he had arrived clothed. He wasn't sure what he would have done if he'd turned up naked – perhaps they would have taken notice of him then.

He decided there was only one thing to do; to attract someone's attention. The adults looked intent on wherever they were headed but little ones were more curious, looking around.

So he decided to try to speak to one of them. They walked in grooves, a few feet apart, never colliding with anyone on the same level, so he stepped out, between an adult and child, making the child stop.

It looked fearful at him then to its parent. The adult hadn't noticed it lagging behind.

"Hello," Alex said.

The 'child' replied, scared, but not in words that had made sense to him.

Finally the parent noticed and came back, angry. They argued, neither of them saying anything that Alex could understand.

The parent put out an arm and touched Alex's forehead with a flat palm. It opened its mouth again and this time he did understand.

"Be on your way. We don't talk to the food."

## Parallel Bars

*A hero doesn't have to rescue people from a burning building. He, or she, doesn't have to develop a miracle cure. Anyone can be a hero and sometimes it takes something very small to been seen as one; a small gesture, small talk, a small step.*

Being told she'd never walk again made Abbie all the more determined. She'd known the risks when she signed up, headed out to a country she could barely spell, in heat she'd not been prepared for.

Sun bathing was nothing compared to this. No sun cream manufacturer made a factor that would go this high but she loved every second, the camaraderie she'd never known, even being one of seven siblings, and it was their strength she found when she got home, badly injured with months of physio training ahead of her.

The two metal poles stretching out reminded her of the parallel bars she'd used at school, except then she'd bounded up to them, performing twists and somersaults like she'd later do in diving competitions.

"Twenty minutes today," Donovan told her nonchalantly as if that would be easy. It had been fifteen minutes yesterday, ten the day before. She'd wanted to give up at five.

He'd let go once she'd grabbed the poles, them supporting her thin frame, then he'd stood back, waiting for her to move. She wanted to cheat, pull her legs along with her hands but she'd tried that, alone in her specially-adapted bedroom, with nothing to support her, and had collapsed in a heap.

Now, she wanted to look around the room at her friends, some newer than others, do anything but walk. Except that's all she wanted to do, just a simple action that so many take for granted, that she had.

"Any time you like," Don said, winking. "We've got all day."

Abbie knew that wasn't true, that his time was precious, that there were others booked in after her.

So she breathed in, until her lungs felt they had no more space, and grunted her way to a slow arduous painful first step.

"Good," Don said, and moved to the end of the beams so unless she looked down or away, he'd been in her line of sight, like an enemy in the warzone. “Don’t stop,” he said when she’d paused too long.

So she took another lungful of air and twisted her body to guide her left foot forward. Her arms were already beginning to ache, so she slacked off her grip and felt herself falling.

“Grab, Abbie!” Don shouted and she grabbed the bars, keeping herself upright.

“Come on,” he said and she repeated her method, putting out her right foot. “Now that wasn’t so difficult was it,” Don said, smiling at her.

“Easy for you to say,” she growled.

“Yes, it is. But you keep doing that and I won’t need to.”

Abbie gritted her teeth and took another step, swinging her hips to aid her momentum. As she edged closer, Don backed away. “I’m not going off the end,” she said, when he’d stopped a few feet away.

“I know but with hips like that you’ll need some room to turn round.”

“You cheeky git!”

“Gets you moving.”

It was then Abbie realised she was at the end of the bars. Remembering her technique from the previous days, she swung herself round, ignoring the pain that shot up her body, and grabbed the bars as her knees started to buckle.

As he walked back to the other end, Don clapped.

Abbie blushed and concentrated on gripping the bars for the return journey… to Donovan, her former comrade, her best friend, husband-to-be.

## Police Escort

Watching the policeman in her rear view mirror, Hope clicked the button to release the central locking and got out the car.

"Surprised you got here at all," he said softly, kicking her flat tyre.

Hope had watched enough TV to know his American accent to be Californian. "Me too," she said, not meaning the car.

"But we'll have you away in no time."

"No hurry," she said and hoped he'd take all day. With the views being him and the sea, she could think of nowhere else she'd rather be.

"Do you have a spare?"

"No," she said, knowing that her model of car didn't come with one. "I thought they had to, by law, but apparently…"

"No problem. You're travelling a bit back-heavy? Got a body in there?" He laughed, exposing brilliant white teeth.

Hope had never been good at spontaneous laughter and didn't think now was the time to try, so just smiled and shook her head. "Moving house."

"Oh, all your worldly possessions?"

"Yes," she said quietly, picturing the heavy old chest that took up most of the boot.

The man stopped smiling.

"I'm sorry."

"It's okay, really it is. New life, new start."

"New man."

Hope didn't reply.

"I'm sorry," he repeated. "Just here to fix your wheel. I'm new… I'll shut up now."

"It's okay, really it's… I've said that already."

"Don't be nervous. It's the uniform, I know, even makes me nervous."

She laughed then, a natural laugh, and enjoyed it.

"That's better," the man said and held out his hand. "Bryan… Josh Bryan."

As Hope looked at him, she imagined him not in his uniform but in a dinner suit, sipping a cocktail that had been shaken not stirred, with a gun tucked discreetly under his jacket.

"I have some stuff in my trunk that'll fix your car… What is it you Brits say? In a jiffy?

Hope laughed again. "We've not said that since Jeeves and Wooster."

"PG Wodehouse. You read?"

"I do… try to, when I have time."

"I love the old ones. Really funny. Not as far back as Jane Austen, the romance, but…"

"You don't like romance?" Hope surprised them both with that question. "I mean, the classics."

"Twentieth century is as old as I get. Still living there, so my wife says."

Hope's shoulders slumped.

"Ex-wife, I should say. She's still in the States. Couldn't see why I would want to live here, but just look… the sea, the beach, the sun…"

"Don't you have all that in California?"

Josh laughed. "How did you know? Oh, the accent. Giveaway, isn't it. We do but it's a different kind of sun. It's… tiring. Anyway, you'll be wanting to go and we do need to fix your car."

"We do."

She watched him go the back of his patrol car, return with a yellow and black can, connect the tube to the air valve then re-inflate the tyre.

"Is that it?" she asked when he screwed the caps back on both the tyre and can.

"Not permanent. Should get you to the gas station."

"Oh."

"Of course, you won't know one, will you? I'm finishing in a minute anyway, you can follow me."

"Really?"

"Sure. There's one just down from the PD… I mean police station, just down the road from the garage not gas station. I said I was new."

Hope smiled. "Thank you for everything. You're very kind."

Josh nodded and they returned to their cars.

Hope followed him at below the speed limit, without the sirens she'd hoped for but knew wouldn't be warranted. It's not every day you get a police escort and she hoped it wouldn't be the last.

## Once the Love's Gone

As it started to wobble, April looked at her husband's tooth and her heart sank. When had things started going wrong? When had he let himself 'go'?

"You really should go to the dentist," she said for the umpteenth time, but had known the answer before she'd spoken.

"It'll come out of its own accord."

She'd given up saying that it didn't need to, that technology had moved on and the sooner… that's as far as she'd ever got.

So she'd sit at the kitchen table reading her book, a half-hour respite until the oven timer would set her back into action.

She'd read about the exotic lives of the film stars she'd only ever see on the television, watched when he was down the pub, too drunk, too busy to take her to the cinema in town.

April had had an exotic life once, before she'd met him, a handsome young farmer at the local dance. She'd spent the summers picking vines in France, liaisons in the Louvre, backpacking around Europe until her money had run out, then home to reality, her parents, college, a real job in an office before the farm became her life.

As she read her book, she heard him shouting at the TV, answers to quiz shows or an early football match. He'd slap his hand down on the chair's arm, hitting wood through the worn-away foam.

It reminded her of when he'd slap her backside, gently in a playful rather than sexual manner, although she'd give anything for either right now. She wondered whose backside he was slapping these days. Cindy and Emilia down The Old Bull would tolerate it, knowing it came with the territory.

Barbara at The Haven actively encouraging, knowing it usually led to higher tips. This had been one of the nails in the Milton marital coffin – the affection and the money divided elsewhere, like an affair without the adultery, April sure of his fidelity despite appearances, his battle with cancer becoming a battle with her – a silent one – the throat cancer that hadn't robbed him of his voice, just his passion.

She knew it was an act with the other women, but it hurt all the same.

"What's for dinner?" he grumbled, shuffling through to get a beer from the fridge.

"Steak and ale pie." April waited for a reaction but none was forthcoming. She'd chosen his favourite as the alcohol in it, she'd added extra to be sure, would assure her of a quiet evening, quiet other than his snoring while slumped in his armchair if he didn't make it to the pub.

April thought back to the day they'd bought the chair, an odd addition to their old two-piece suite.

"But I like it," he'd groaned when she'd suggested something more neutral, the pattern of the suite long discontinued. She'd thought the armchair hideous but over the years it had hidden the stains of the beer and meals he'd taken through then rushed to eat, eager to meet 'the lads' down the pub, the lads being Ernie and Bert who'd still be eating their dinners, while chatting with their wives, long after he'd arrived so he'd spend his time letching at the bimbos, his loose tooth wobbling in its socket, not bothering anyone but April.

She wondered if that meant she still cared but if she now enjoyed seeing him in pain… was it enjoyment or pity?

She couldn't put her finger on it but one thing she knew was that it was no longer concern, no longer love and once the love's gone, there are decisions to be made, actions to be taken and she knew she had to be the one to make them.

## The Ghost Of The Half-Empty Bed

"You look knackered," they say and you certainly feel like it. Six-hour sleeps certainly haven't done you any favours.

"Early night tonight," you mumble to yourself unconvincingly.

Life's never been quite the same since Doris died, and the void is so big that you think you'll never get over it. Still, you plod on, doing your best. It's just a shame that it's not quite good enough.

Night times are the worst. The bed seems huge without her petite frame lying next to you and the house is too quiet. Your brother Stuart says that you should have moved on by now but what would he know? He still has Jane. He might think about the possibility, but he couldn't know what it's like to lose a soulmate. How it feels now you're only a half.

Unbearable, that's what it is, and you do wonder why you carry on, but the little voice, Doris's, tells you that you have to, so you do it for her.

You think Christmases are going to be the worst but as soon as you're widowed, everyone thinks you'll hate to be on your own, so the invitations flood in. Having people around takes your mind off the day-to-day.

At least there's the dog to be walked. Nolan's getting a bit slow but he'll see out another year or two. "Good company," you imagine Doris saying. She's the company you really want. He was her dog not yours but you look after him all the same.

The alarm finally goes off and you look up. Nolan's there, as always, lying at the end of the bed; on Doris's side. He looks as miserable as you do, and you smile sympathetically. He doesn't notice; still fast asleep, and you laugh at his twitching legs. He won't hear you, of course; deaf as a foghorn, just like Doris.

Nolan reacts to movement these days, so you edge out of the bed, slowly pulling back the sheets.

You imagine Doris shaking her head. She'd upgraded to a duvet years ago but it never suited you. With Doris's shifting and Nolan's weight, you always ended up with a cold side.

You didn't like to complain because Doris always had other things to think about, but now you'd give anything to swap the sheets for her. You treated yourself, gave the duvet to the animal refuge, but the sheets aren't how you remember them.

You no longer have a cold side but you're not warm either; the ghost of the half-empty bed sees to that.

You walk to the window and peek through a gap in the curtains. You think that anyone seeing them move will misjudge you, now you're on your own. You no longer have a wife to hide behind; just curtains.

The snow that started falling the previous night is now as thick as a doorstop and your heart sinks. But then you smile. Stuart's house is going to be impassable in this weather and he'll be too busy with his children building a snowman to think about collecting you.

You'll have phoned to say you'll stay locally and imagine the smile on his face as he realises he can have a beer or two after scooping up his children when they refuse to come in for lunch.

You will stay locally, very locally. You'll share the sofa with Nolan, something else Doris would have frowned at, wading your way through turkey and trimmings for one.

You'll open a big bottle of malt which you'll raise to the health of the Queen. Yours isn't so good these days but you don't complain. You'll wait for Nolan then have your early night and look for Doris's smile.

Morgen Bailey

## Sabbatical From The Rat Race

As Sandy plodded up the hill, she debated what would be over the summit in a 'loves me, loves me not' fashion. "Houses, nothing, houses, nothing." She wanted houses but all the hills so far had produced just luscious green valleys, a welcoming sight in any other circumstance but a week of just green had made it lose its appeal.

A week of no company since she'd had to leave Adriel behind.

It hadn't been her idea. For all she knew, they were the only two humans left but they'd both known he'd not last another night so she'd left him with the gun and the solitary bullet.

She knew the shot was coming but even so, hearing it had been the worst moment in her life. That and the disease that had spread the planet almost instantly.

She'd seen the films 'I Am Legend', 'The Road', and 'Contagion', so knew it was possible, but of course would never happen in real life. Except it had. And she'd been one of the few, like Will Smith, who'd been immune to whatever it was. 'The few,' she laughed. Her.

It had been her idea to move to the country, those weeks before, to live a life of solitude, to finish the novel that had been taunting her, Adriel to take a sabbatical from the rat race, just a radio for company, and to live hundreds of miles from a living soul, or not living as the case may be.

Her rucksack was getting heavier every step and sometimes she'd drag it behind her but the material had thinned, the contents threatening to escape. The water and snacks she knew would only last a couple more days and after that, she had no plan.

She'd never been a planner and this she reasoned was why she'd struggled with her novel until they'd moved there, and the words flowed like the waterfall they'd discovered on their first walk through the woods surrounding their cabin.

The waterfall had filled the bottles they'd carried with them until it had made Adriel sick.

Just a few more feet and she'd know. She stopped, stood upright and listened. Hoping for life, human or otherwise. Put in extreme circumstances and a person will do anything, kill anything… or anyone, if it meant life or death. But she heard nothing so carried on walking to the brow of the hill, expecting to see nothing but land, so wanted to scream when she saw a house. Just one but one was enough. If it was empty, it would be shelter. If it was occupied, she'd take her chance that they were friendly, equally pleased to see her as her them.

She wanted to run down the hill, arms flailing, but common sense and the past few days had taught her caution. She waited, watched for signs of life.

Apart from smoke from the chimney, there was nothing. No vehicle, no animals, no birds. Much as she wanted to get to the house as quickly as she could, she sat down to think.

She'd been anticipating human life over every hilltop but now there could be some, she wasn't sure what she should do, so she thought scenarios; the best that could happen, the worst.

When she'd worked out all the options, she stood and started walking, slowly, ready to drop to the ground at any sign of movement, her dark clothes camouflaging her enough to buy her some time.

As she reached the bottom of the hill and onto flat land, she felt exposed, with no trees to hide behind, no shelter of any kind, she walked quicker, until she stumbled on an obstinate stone. Distracted, she looked up at the house as the door opened.

## Only A Figure Of Speech

"In the car please, Amara."

"Have you got my gym kit?"

"In the back."

"And my trip form."

"Mara! Hurry up and get in. I want to have a word with you about Chuck."

"My form, Mum."

"In your school bag."

"The holdall?"

"No, your school bag, the red one. Did you pick your lunch off the kitchen table?"

"Of course."

"So we can go now, yes?"

"Yep."

"Then put on your seatbelt."

"Oh, hold on."

"What?"

"Holly wanted me to bring my DS."

"But you're seeing her tonight."

"She might not be able to come."

"What?"

"I forgot, she has violin on a Tuesday."

"But you asked."

"I forgot."

"Let me know at lunchtime, okay?"

"Oops."

"What now?"

"My mobile's on the kitchen table."

"What? Why?"

"I had to put it down to put the lunch in my bag."

"Amara! It's too late to go back now, so use Holly's."

"She doesn't have one."

"Oh, okay. You can borrow mine but you're not to lose it or Dad will kill you."

"He will?"

"Of course not. It's only a figure of speech."

"Then why did you say it?"

"Amara. I'll give you my phone. Dad won't kill you if you lose it, but just don't, okay?"

"Is it an expensive phone?"

"Valuable to me, yes. Lots of numbers on it. I didn't know Holly played the violin."

"Level two."

"Very good. How did Chuck seem to you this morning?"

"Fine."

"Just fine?"

"You know. Like always."

"Not quieter? Subdued?"

"What's that?"

"Subdued. It means quiet."

"English is stupid."

"What have you got first thing?"

"Art."

"That's nice, you like art."

"We're making collages out of magazine pictures."

"Do you get to bring them home?"

"Oh."

"Oh?"

"We're supposed to bring in some magazines."

"Child! How did you get so forgetful?"

"Dad says I take after him."

"You do. And Chuck. Why didn't he leave a note?"

"Because he told me. Can we stop by the store?"

"We don't have time, you know that."

"But I need some magazines."

"Oh, alright but two minutes, no more."

"You wait here and I'll get a random selection, okay?"

"Okay, Mum. Can you leave the radio on?"

"Sure."

"And can you get some ice cream?"

"I'm not going straight home after dropping you off, it'll melt."

"Chocolate then. Chocolate chocolate. White chocolate chocolate?"

"Okay. But none to take to school. It'll come home with me."

"I thought you weren't going home."

"Not straight away, no."

"Where are you going?"

"I'm going to have a word with Mr Francome."

"The Principal?"

"Yes. Just a quick word."

"About me?"

"No, Amara, not about you."

"Chuck then. What's he done?"

"I don't know, Amara. Nothing, I think, but…"

"There's a space there, Mum, right by the store entrance."

"Alright then. How many magazines do you need?"

"Three or four, I guess. I don't know."

"I'll get four then any you don't chop up I can read."

"These are grown-ups magazines, mum."

"You're making a collage, aren't you?"

"Yes."

"There's all sorts in there. You'll be spoilt for choice."

"But it's cooking… and fashion… and stuff."

"What's the matter with that?"

"It's supposed to be about monsters?"

"Monsters? You didn't tell me monsters."

"Didn't I?"

"Count to ten…"

"One… two…"

"No, not you, Amara."

"But you said…"

"Just a figure of speech."

"Okay, we're here. Don't forget your gym stuff in the back."

"Mum!"

"Have a good day."

"Why are you going to see Mr Francome?"

"I've told you. You're late. Go… shoo."

"Bye, Mum."

"Hi. Is Mr Francome free, please?"

"Hello. Do you have an appointment?"

"I don't. Sorry. It's a spur of the moment thing."

"Can I tell him what it's about?"

"I'd just like to have a quick word about my son."

"And your name…"

"Chuck? What are you doing here?"

## Chalk and Fromage

It was during the day trip to France that had started the divorce, or at least Claire's thinking of it. It was his whistling that she thought sounded like a Eurovision tune; one that had scored 'nul points'… or worse. She knew that wasn't possible but this was a song she'd heard a dozen times that morning, as he was packing the car, and the repetitive melody grated.

The image of French cheese being slid monotonously down a grater made her feel hungry and knowing they'd arrive in Paris around lunchtime, she was looking forward to a large bottle of rosé with brie and French bread, the rosé being hers as he'd insist on driving.

Paris was one of the most romantic cities in the world but another 'city' had crushed what little they'd had in their marriage: Manchester City – every home and away game in the seven years they'd been together.

They'd even timed their wedding around the football season two years later. Saturdays between August and May had become her clothes shopping or spa days; also making sure she was busy when he checked the results on the TV despite having seen the game live.

"The cameras spot me sometimes," he'd say, justifying his second-by-second analysis of the late-night highlights.

Chalk and cheese, she thought as he drove the car on to the ferry and handed the tickets back to her for safekeeping.

She smiled at him, hoping for a flash of affection but none was forthcoming.

It's her repetitive moaning I can't stand so I hum it out with a little tune I know. And it sounds nicer as a whistle… like a bird. That's what she used to say anyway.

It was her idea to go to France. I don't even like the French; they're… well, French. She thinks it'll be romantic; like our honeymoon… better than our honeymoon, but then you can't get much worse than Hurricane George on the not-so-tropical island of Mongoose. Mongoon it is of course but it'll always be Mongoose to me after that; watching those birds from the sanctuary being swept away.

Holidays weren't really the same after that. We stayed on dry land. British soil. I've always been the traveller but kept my mouth shut for her. Well, I didn't get a look in, did I?

She was so quiet when we first met; that was… seven years ago now. And this is why we're here; our fifth anniversary is next week, except she couldn't get the time off work so we're just away for the weekend. Out of season of course.

I said I wouldn't have minded waiting; the football season is only on from August to May. A saint she is… of course, but she acts like it's martyrdom sometimes. But then she likes the sun and June July is normally pretty nice isn't it.

Yeah, that's what we thought when we booked it… I got drenched just loading the car. A 'baby' she called me… used to call me that in a nice way but then when we were told we couldn't actually have a real one… you know, a baby baby, she stopped saying it. Topic non-grata or whatever the saying is.

Didn't help that it was my fault. "It's no one's fault," she'd said but she looked at me funny, and never really looked at me the same way again.

But they got it wrong. Gibson I want to call him, after Tait, one of my heroes, but she was having none of it. Kendal, she wants. I ask you. Kendal. She's always had this thing about the Peak District and those Kardashians.

I really like Felicity Kendal but I'm not having my child named after a slab of mint cake or a Z-lister, but then she just looks at me funny. The wife, not Felicity, unfortunately.

Oh dear, she's pulling that face – must be wind again.

## Talking When We Could Be Walking

"Oh no! Is it really eleven already?"

"You've got plenty of time."

"Dad, I'm supposed to be there at midday."

"It's only a ten-minute drive. Fifty minutes easily."

"I don't want to be there on the dot! I want to be a bit early."

"Brides aren't supposed to be early. It's tradition."

"I certainly don't want to be late. What time is the car booked for?"

"Eleven. You know that. It's downstairs, but we have it until it drops you and Jude at the reception."

"Have you spoken to Jude today?"

"No, Suzie. Why would I?"

"Just to check that everything's okay."

"It'll be fine. Stop panicking."

"Something's going to go wrong. I can feel it."

"Nothing's going to go wrong. You're a secretary. Everything's precision-timed."

"But I should have been ready by now."

"You look ready to me and you look gorgeous. Your mother would have–"

"Dad, don't! You'll set me off and Vita's done my make-up."

"Is there anything else to do?"

"Erm… no, I don't think so."

"Okay. So you're ready. The bridesmaids are ready."

"The bridesmaids! How are they getting there?"

"Uncle Terry's taking them. You know that. Don't panic."

"Oh, yes. Sorry. I know. I'm making–"

"A mountain out of a proverbial molehill. It's your prerogative but just enjoy the day."

"Okay. Thanks, Dad."

"What was that noise?"

"A bad gear change, I think. Nothing to worry about. The driver knows what he's doing."

"I knew we should have left earlier."

"But then we'd be too early and we'd be driving round in circles."

"You're right as alw– What was that?"

"It didn't sound good."

"We're slowing down! There's smoke!"

"Oh dear. Never mind, we'll get a lift with Uncle Terry and the bridesmaids."

"Everyone else has left already."

"So he'll be available to come and get you. Ring him on your mobile."

"I don't have my mobile, Dad. Wedding dresses don't come with pockets."

"But you've got a bag."

"Horseshoe, flowers. Two hands so no, no bag. I told you you should get a phone."

"Never needed one. You only live round the corner."

"Oh, Dad. What are we going to do?"

"Maybe the driver's… no? That's ridic– You'd think he'd have some way of communicating with his company. How is he supposed to tell them…? We'll have to walk. We've got time."

"It's at least a mile."

"We've got half an hour. Twenty minutes a mile."

"Maybe we can find a phone box."

"Have you got change?"

"No. I told you, no pockets. Don't tell me you don't have any."

"I've only brought my wallet. Notes and cards."

"So you've got money."

"We're sitting here talking when we could be walking."

"I'm going to cry."

"Don't. Vita's done your make-up. Come on. If we chat while we're walking we'll be there in no time."

"Thanks, Dad."

"That's what I'm here for. It's alright, Wallace. Not your fault. We'll make our own way but please be there when we come out. Okay? Thanks."

"Oh, God."

"What?"

"I didn't think about getting to the reception."

"Don't worry, Suzie. We can take Uncle Terry's car. There'll be plenty of other people who can take the bridesmaids."

"This is not how I had it planned."

"I know but as long as you get there."

"These shoes are killing me already. I only needed to walk–"

"What?"

"The police car's stopping. You don't think…"

"You never know."

"He's getting out, opening the back door. Yes, Dad!"

"Hello, officer. St Barnaby. The car broke… It's very kind of you."

"Yes. Thank you!"

"Thank you again, officer."

"Thank you so much."

"Hurry, Dad!"

"It's five to. We're fine. Slow down. Breathe."

"Yes, Dad. Okay. Calm, Suzie… calm."

"Step… step… three… four… There's the music. We're here. We've arrived. You're going to get married."

"Look! There's Jude. Doesn't she look lovely?"

"Yes, Suzie. Suit and all, but yes, she looks lovely."

## Feeding the Father

"There we go, Dad," I say, putting down the bowl of jelly. Dad don't say much these days. In fact we ain't spoken for weeks. He just stares at the TV. 'Neighbours' coming up...his favourite.

I don't mind doing everything. He and mum looked after me for years so now it's my turn but sometimes it gets a bit lonely, just talking to myself.

Dad looks smart today. I put him in his favourite jumper, the blue one. I can't change his trousers as he's too heavy but it don't matter as he don't go nowhere. I must get him some more aftershave as he don't smell too good.

Things started going wrong after Mum left. If she hadn't gone, everything would be alright. Said she couldn't take it no more. I know she meant me. Blames me for being stupid. They had rows. Know they had no money 'cause they had to look after me. So, now it's my turn. Look after my dad.

He's not hungry tonight – left his food again. He's not been hungry for a while. "Need your strength Dad," I say but he just stares at the TV, looks straight through me.

There's the doorbell. Don't answer 'cause it's nobody's business. I can manage just fine on my own. But then I'm not on my own – I got Dad. I turn the TV up loud when they start shouting through the letterbox. If I can't hear them then they can't hear me... us. Not that Dad says anything. He don't seem to mind people shouting at him. I never shout at him. I love him, see.

The letterbox voices have gone quiet.

'Neighbours' starts and I laugh. "Everybody needs good neighbours" the voices sing to me. Well we don't. Neighbours are nosey. Shouting and banging on the walls. We keep us-selves to us-selves. Don't need no one sticking their beaks into our business.

When the banging starts again, I shut the lounge door. Thump...thump...thump. I feel the room shake then there's a crash. Voices! The lounge door bursts open and I look at the faces. One man looks at Dad and gasps. Dad don't look back, he's too busy staring at 'Neighbours'.

One of the men grabs me to take me out the room, but I don't wanna go. Can't leave Dad… he needs me. Another man goes upstairs and shouts down, "The mother's up here." There's no one up there. I know. Mum left us, she ain't there. It's just Dad and me. Me and Dad.

I get bundled in a van and taken to hospital. I don't like hospitals. Went there when I was seven when I broke my arm. It hurt. And they kept poking my arm to see how much it hurt. Couldn't they see it did 'cause I was crying? Don't need no doctors and neither does Dad. He's got me, he don't need no one else.

They sit me in a chair and give me a cup of tea with lots of sugar. I like it, it's sweet. Then they start talking.

Did I know my dad was dead? "Course he ain't dead," I say. Dad just likes watching TV. I feed him so he don't need to go nowhere.

Then they talk about mum. I don't want to talk about her, 'cause she left us. They ask me when I saw her last and I say it was my birthday, fifteenth August. Dad said I was sixty, but I ain't that old. No one's that old.

I tell them Mum left 'cause I was hard work. I know I was hard work but not anymore. I do the work. I look after Dad. That's what I do.

The man left the room and I heard him talking to someone. Then he came back in and brought me here. I like it here, apart from the voices, but I miss my dad.

"Mister, when can I see my dad?"

## The Big Black One with the Space in the Back

I can't breathe… I… can't… breathe… Help.

I want to shout but I can't speak. It's too hot in here. I'm going to cook. Someone, please, look at me, see what's happening. I try to cough out the words but all I do is cough.

Yes! He's looking… I know him! He's Mr Langley from that funeral place on Rawlings Terrace. He's measuring me up for a coffin, I can tell, it's in his eyes.

"Hello, Mateo."

Cough. "Hello…" Breathe. "Mr Langley."

"You don't look very well. Are you okay?"

I decide that nodding is the best thing to do.

He smiles and I think he really means it. He doesn't seem disappointed at all that I'm all right. "What are you reading?"

I look down at the book, my dad's dictionary, and blush. He doesn't know I've got it and he doesn't like me taking things without asking, so I turn it over so Mr Langley can't see the front.

"Just a school book," I lie, and he nods.

"Are you sure you're okay?"

I nod again and add a smile this time.

"Okay. Well… they'll get the bus running in a minute. And if they don't they'll send another one."

Oh God. We're going to have to wait? That could take hours.

Breathe. Mum tells me not to panic, that I should breathe. I'm trying, but all I do is gulp air like a goldfish and some of it goes down the wrong way so I cough again.

I want Mr Langley to return to his seat but he doesn't.

"Do you mind if I sit next to you, Matty?"

I shake my head. Mum says I shouldn't talk to strangers but Dad knows him, pointed him out to me once, so he must be all right, and there are lots of people around.

"It'll be nice to have the company, if I'm honest," he says to me. If he's honest? Does that mean he's not? If they do 'get the bus running', will he follow me if I get off alone? Will he…

"Makes me nervous," he continues.

I don't know what he's got to be nervous about, unless he doesn't travel on the bus very often. He's not been on mine before. “Nervous? Why?”

“Can you keep a secret?”

I look at my dad’s dictionary and nod.

“I don’t like confined spaces,” he tells me.

I want to open the dictionary but don’t. “What’s confined?” I ask him.

“It’s being in a small space when you want to be in a big one.”

It’s nice to know he feels like I do, so I grin like my dad does when my mum’s just kissed him. “But this is a bus, it’s big.”

“I know,” he says and laughs.

“And you’re not alone,” I add.

He nods. I feel a bit better but he doesn’t look so good now. I wait for him to carry on but he doesn’t. “Why did you get on the bus if you don't like being here?” I know it’s a silly question because I did the same thing but I have to because Mum and Dad are working.

“My car’s being serviced.”

“The big black one with the space in the back for…”

He laughs again. “Yes, Matty, the hearse. I’m on my way to collect it now.”

I’m too young for a car but I know Mum and Dad love driving theirs. It must be horrible for him not to have one, especially one that’s so special.

The bus wobbles and someone behind me cheers. Mr Langley looks happy too and makes me feel good.

“The garage is on the way to your house, Matty, I could give you a lift, save you being on this thing the whole journey.”

I’ve always wanted to travel in a hearse. Hearse. Confined. I’ve learned two new words today. I don’t think my dad will mind at all.

## Curved Into A Smile

Tommy-Lee Forté shook his head as the screen announced the next caller: Nigel Allibone. Dull. Forty-watt bulbs were brighter.

A consumer slot was not what Tommy had envisaged for his career in radio but it paid the bills, handsomely in fact. Consumer issues encouraged dull, and Tommy knew all about that, having been born Benedict Egglington, Benedict after his paternal grandfather. Tommy's younger brother, Rico, a Mötley Crüe fan, had got off lightly.

Tommy looked up at the perspex separating him and his producer, Sandy, but she looked down at her desk, jotting something in a message book.

Tommy flicked a switch and announced, "You're back with T-Lee's Consumer Hour, and next we have one of our regular callers, Nigel from Kindlingbury-on-Sea. Good afternoon, Nigel, and how are you today?" Tommy winced as Nigel sneezed into his earpiece. "Bless you."

A cold-ridden Nigel mumbled a 'thank you'.

"What would you like to talk about today?"

"Erm… I don't really know how to begin."

"Come now, Nigel. You know me. Nothing is taboo, or too much trouble, on my show." Tommy flicked back a dark strand of gelled hair. "We're all family, here at Furze FM."

"I know but–"

"Go on, anything you like. You have a problem, we'll sort it out. Not failed you yet, have we, Nigel?"

"No… you haven't. Alright then," Nigel blurted, before blowing his nose. "Ann Summers! I bought… er, bought something from them and it broke, and they won't give me a refund or exchange like they should. They said I broke it, that I was too… er, forceful with it."

Tommy looked up at Sandy. Unlike him, she couldn't see the funny side.

She made no attempt though to stop Nigel talking, to cut him off, but sat impassively on the other side of the screen, waiting to see what Tommy and his caller were going to say next.

"Hello?" Nigel asked the silent studio.

"Sorry, Nigel," Tommy said. "I was just lining up the next song. I daren't ask what you bought but it doesn't really matter because if an item's not fit for purpose then the shop should–"

"I bought a butt–"

"Okay. Well, as I… er, as I said, the item is irrelevant but I'm sure we can contact the store for you and get this sorted. Thank you, Nigel, as always, for calling in. We have your number and will get back to you. And now we have Beyoncé and… er, *Single Ladies (Put a Ring on It)*."

Tommy flicked two switches on the panel in front of him, cutting off Nigel and starting the music. Then he looked up at impassive-Sandy. "What an asshole, no pun intended. Actually, pun very much intended."

He waited for her to say something but she didn't move, so he continued. "Anyone sad enough to get one of those things, or even go to Ann Summers in the first place, must be pretty desperate, or lonely, or both…"

He waited for a nod, shake of the head, a shrug, but again nothing. Her reactions were rarely positive where he was concerned, so he should have known better.

"I mean…" He was going to continue but knew it was pointless so sat in silence waiting for Sandy to connect the next call.

As Beyoncé belted out her final chorus, Sandy pointed to her mid-air microphone then towards him.

Tommy looked at his microphone but saw nothing untoward, then looked at the button connecting it, and the callers, to the rest of the world.

"Oh God," he whispered and went pale. The button he'd tapped to disconnect Nigel hadn't been to the mic but an obsolete button which had done nothing since they'd stopped using vinyl.

Sandy smiled as a little voice squeaked, "I'm still here, you know." Sandy held her manicured right index finger up to the left side of her neck.

Tommy gulped as she drew an invisible line, and her red-lipsticked mouth curved into a smile.

## Phonetics – A Winter's Tale

"What the–!"

"Sorry! Oh God, I'm so sorry. Me and my bovver boots."

"Shh…"

"Sorry. Is your foot okay?"

"Fine."

"I'm so… I couldn't sleep last night and had nothing to read so…"

"Nothing?"

"No."

"You don't keep any books in the house?"

"Flat."

"Not even classics?"

"No."

"Shakespeare."

"Nope."

"The Bible, then. Everyone has a Bible."

"God, no… Sorry, are you?"

"You say 'sorry' a lot."

"I do, yes."

"Divorced?"

"How did you know? Oh, saying 'sorry'. It used to work…"

"That's a shame."

"Not really."

"So you have plenty of time to read."

"Not really. I'm always on the motorway, or sleeping."

"Sorry?"

"It's catching."

"What?"

"Never mind."

"You're on the road a lot? Salesman?"

"Maintenance. On the motorway. You know, all the smart ones."

"Oh yes. And you work from the minute you get there 'til you finish?"

"No, there are lunch breaks, other breaks… when it's raining. This is England."

"Perfect."

"For…"

"Reading."

"Suppose, but I'm with the lads."

"You can't get away?"

"Not really. The porta cabins are noisy and the motorway's… noisy. Besides, they'll think I'm a… you know."

"Does it matter?"

"Don't suppose so."

"How many of you are there?"

"Forty. Fifty maybe."

"Wow. You could…"

"I could…?"

"Start a book group?"

"I don't think so. They're very macho, my lot."

"You could ask."

"I guess. You like reading, don't you. Big stack of books you've got there. They allow you that many at once?"

"I have two cards."

"Isn't that a bit greedy."

"Not both mine."

"Old man's?"

"Yes."

"Large print. Very old man."

"Yes. Neighbour."

"Sorry, being nosey."

"You weren't going to say 'sorry' again."

"I wasn't? Force of habit. While I'm being nosey, and getting away with it…"

"You were?"

"I thought so, but…"

"Go on."

"What do you do that lets you read so much? The old man… you a carer?"

"No."

"Librarian."

"Not even close."

"Indoors though."

"Mostly."

"For a company."

"Yes."

"You're very…"

"What?"

"Skinny."

"Naturally slim."

"I should pick my book and go… before I get a parking ticket."

"What are you going for? The book."

"Something with action, shortish chapters."

"James Patterson's are short, about one or two pages mostly."

"That's ridiculous."

"He's very popular. Most borrowed… or stolen, can't remember which."

"People's steal from libraries?"

"I meant bookshops but yes, they probably do."

"Isn't that pointless? Aren't they free?"

"They are but you need a card."

"Which is free, or at least mine was."

"They are. So you've guessed I work for a company, indoors and I'm skinny. What do I do?"

"Secretary."

"Are secretaries skinny?"

"Not necessarily."

"Okay, clue…"

"Your foot. You're a chiropodist."

"Nope."

"Treading on a spot. You squash spiders. Bug exterminator."

"No. I'm going to have to tell you."

"One more clue."

"Swan Lake."

"You make matches."

"No. That's Swan Vesta. I don't even smoke."

"Me neither. Disgusting habit. Swan Lake… conservationist… no… oh, man in black tights… baddie, dark music. Yes. Ballerina. Of course."

"We're going through early rehearsals at the moment so plenty of time to read."

"Where are you playing?"

"At the Royal, do you know it?"

"The wife… ex, took me there once. It was funny. Graham Greene, I think. Not somewhere to go on your own though."

"Why not?"

"I don't know. It's just… I don't know. Never think of it, I suppose, like reading."

"Step on a Crack."

"Sorry?"

"James Patterson. Michael Letwidge. It's very good."

"Okay, thanks. And sorry about your foot."

"No more 'sorries', okay?"

"I'll try."

"And come to the ballet. You might enjoy it."

"Sure. What are you doing?"

"You wouldn't know it, it's a bit of a classic."

"Try me."

"It's Shakespeare."

"Oh."

"Haven't you got to get back to your car?"

"My car! I didn't even catch your name…"

"Juliet. Bye then."

"Bye, Juliet."

As Mike walked away, he wanted to turn, go back, ask for her number, give her his but she wouldn't have taken him seriously had she known, that despite everything, he's romantic, that he's half-Italian, told her the real reason his colleagues make fun of him… that his surname is Romeo.

## They Try To With The Food

*(written as a homage to Roald Dahl)*

"Cherry Pie, Keith?"

"Yes, Marilyn."

"No stones?"

"No, Marilyn."

"Thank you, Keith."

"You're welcome."

"Oh yes… it's still warm. Well done you."

"Shall I put the kettle on?"

"That would be lovely."

"Right you are."

Marilyn knew the pie would taste even better with the tea but didn't want it to get cold so took a bite and savoured it until she heard the kettle boil.

"Are you not having any tea, Keith?"

"I have to go back to work."

"This late?"

"We're a doctor down so I've been seeing more patients, more paperwork. Don't wait up."

Had Marilyn looked out the window or waved her husband goodbye from the front door, she would have seen him turn left instead of right as he should have done to go to the surgery. Of course Keith knew she'd still be sitting on the sofa as she did every Monday and Thursday evening when he brought her cherry pie.

"Oh, Keith!"

"Oh, Sheila!"

"That was wonderful."

"It was."

"When are you going to leave Marilyn?"

"Soon."

"How soon?"

"Soon, my darling."

"You know I have a business trip next week."

"I do and I shall miss you dreadfully."

"You will?"

"Of course. You know I only want to be with you."

"Then leave her."

"I shall."

"While I'm away. If you've not left her when I come back, then we're over."

"Sheila!"

"I mean it."

"Okay."

"Okay?"

"Yes, my darling."

"You will?"

"I will."

"While I'm away?"

"Yes."

"Oh, Keith!"

"Oh, Sheila!"

"Hello, McNeill."

"Hello, Doctor Castle."

"Do you have what I asked for?"

"I do, sir. You did want this strength, didn't you?"

"I did."

"They're quite lethal in the wrong hands."

"Just as well they're in mine."

"Fair point. There we are then."

"Thank you, McNeill."

"Good day, sir."

"I'm home!"

"Goodie. Do you have it?"

"I have, Marilyn, still warm."

"Thank you, dear."

"You're welcome."

"Work again, tonight?"

"Not tonight, no. I thought I might go to the club though."

"You do work so hard."

"You don't mind?"

"Not at all. There's a really good programme about dung beetles just about to start."

"That's nice, dear. I'll make you a cup of tea first though, yes?"

"Not tonight, Keith, not thirsty."

"Alright then."

"…Not hungry either," she said when she heard the front door slam.

The program it turned out was less interesting than Marilyn had hoped and she'd swiftly fallen asleep only to be disturbed by a visitor who hadn't stayed long.

"It's last orders, Doctor Castle, would you like another?"

"Better not, Derek."

"Will we be seeing you tomorrow for the bridge match?"

"I'm not sure. I'll know better when I get home."

"Not a problem, Doctor Castle. Have a good night, sir."

"Thank you, Derek."

Keith Castle eased the key into the door and let himself into his house and crept into the lounge. He smiled when he saw his wife sprawled across the sofa, eyes firmly shut. He looked at the coffee table and saw no pie.

He was leaning over her when her eyes sprang open and she screamed. He backed away just as violently.

"Keith! What were you doing?"

"Oh God! Er… sorry, Marilyn. I thought I saw…"

"What?"

"I don't know, something moving, I'm not sure."

"Where?"

"I think it's gone."

"Thank goodness."

"Was your pie nice?"

"I don't know."

"Oh? You've not eaten it yet?"

"I wasn't hungry."

"Never mind. You could have it now. I'll put the kettle on."

"No need."

"For lunch tomorrow then."

"If you buy me another."

"Sorry?"

"I wasn't hungry so I gave it away."

"Gave… gave it away? There was… someone here?"

"Only for a few minutes. Was in a hurry. Had to catch a plane."

"Really?"

"A business trip, she said."

Keith swallowed hard. "She?"

"Oh, yes. Sheila, one of your colleagues. Said she wanted an update on something…"

"And you gave her the pie?"

"I didn't think you'd mind. I wasn't hungry and you know what aeroplane food is like. If they don't kill you with the turbulence, they try to with the food."

## Small Town Drama

Broadville didn't exactly follow the Trades Description Act. When it was first laid out in the nineteen hundreds, it consisted of a straight road, ten houses, a shop, and thirty-three residents; nineteen adults and fourteen children. Over a century later, it was still one road, ten houses and a shop but twenty-four residents and a pub. It didn't make much money but being a self-sufficient community, they muddled along.

That is until a stranger came to town.

"Excuse me, are you lost?"

"I don't think so."

"On your way somewhere?"

"Not particularly."

"There aren't any houses for sale here."

"That's okay, I'm not looking."

Gary Tindell was stumped. No one came to Broadville unless they were visiting and being the oldest resident, he knew this guy wasn't here for that. He also figured that asking more questions wouldn't bring anything but trouble, so he smiled, tipped his hat and went off to the pub for his evening constitutional.

As he approached the pub's front door, he glanced back and saw the man heading for the shop. With no way for the stranger to see Gary without turning round, Gary waited and watched him go inside.

Gary waited some more. And waited. And waited. He was a pretty patient chap; he'd nursed his wife through cancer, even endured the soaps on TV while she endured the treatment. The pub's opening hours were dependent upon who wanted serving so he had plenty of time to kill.

Thinking that he must have missed him, though not sure how, Gary was about to go into the pub when the man came out of the shop. Gary snuck behind a pillar and pretended to text on a mobile phone. He didn't have one and was just tapping into his palm but the stranger wouldn't know that.

Gary laughed quietly at getting one over on him. Except the man wouldn't have known that either, because he wasn't looking. He was chatting to Elver, the owner of the shop, Gary's less-than-honest brother-in-law.

Gary watched them shake hands. That wasn't good. He knew saying anything to Elver would prove fruitless but Elver talked to his wife, Gary's sister, and she spoke to Gary's wife, so Gary would just have to bide his time.

He didn't have to wait long.

The following evening when he returned from the pub, Dixie put his favourite meal in front of him. Shepherd's pie. He loved the intricate plough-lines she'd weave into the topping. Her smile was extra perky as she placed the dish in front of him.

"Had a good day, dear?" he asked.

"Oh, you know, the same as usual."

"That's good, dear. So nothing special happened then."

"Not really," she said hesitantly, but then pulled out the chair opposite him and slumped into it. Gary stared at her as her eyes worked out how to tell him the news.

Since she'd lost her hair, her pale green eyes had become even more noticeable, he hoped they wouldn't lose any of their shine as her baby-soft blonde fuzz grew back.

"You know something, don't you?" she asked.

"Not really."

"You do, I can tell."

"I saw a guy go into Elver's shop last night and…"

"You did? What was he like?"

"Rude."

"You spoke to him?"

"Briefly. Did Elver say what he wanted?"

Her smile broadened to a grin. "You'll never guess."

Guessing was one thing that Gary was particularly bad at, and Dixie knew that. "A film shoot," she blurted.

"Really?" Flashes of Charlize Theron, Angelina Jolie and Mila Kunis ran through his brain.

"Well, not film," Dixie added.

Gary deflated.

"The small screen."

*That's okay*, Gary thought, *lots of movies are shown on TV these days.*

"Emmerdale," she continued. "They want to use our little town to do a specific scene."

"Really?" he asked, salvaging some enthusiasm and thinking he might even get a walk-on part.

"Yes," she nodded and grinned. "Elver thinks it's a plane crash… or did he say train?"

*Oh great*, Gary thought, *as if I haven't had enough drama in my life.*

## The Houseguest

Odelle wasn't a party person. One thing she was though was neighbourly, and a party to welcome a neighbour's friend sounded as if it might be alright. "Mexico? Where Gloria lives? Does she speak English?"

"Pretty sure she does," Odelle's husband had assured her. "Sounds like fun, shame I'll miss it."

"You will?"

"Camilla wants me in for a few hours."

"Brian! I can't go on my own."

"Why not? You'll know everyone there. It's only for the street."

"But I don't speak Mexican."

"Spanish."

"You know I'm not good with languages, Brian."

"But you're good with people, dear. Speak slowly, clearly, with lots of hand gestures and you'll be fine. Practice for when your sister visits."

"But that's six months away and she'll still be able to speak English." Odelle paused. "She will, won't she? Twelve years isn't long enough to forget, is it?"

Brian shook his head so Odelle turned the conversation back to the party. "And they've given us no notice. I haven't really got anything to wear."

"How about your anniversary dress? That's pretty."

"But that's for us."

"And the other diners in the restaurant."

"I suppose so, but…"

"But?"

"Well…"

"You go, dear. You'll have a great time. Think of me, stuck in front of a boring computer."

"And what about food?"

"Just a sandwich will be fine. And I can make it."

"No, I mean to take with me. Won't they expect me to take something?"

"It's normally bring a bottle but if you did want to."

"There's a Banoffee pie in the freezer."

"Perfect. My favourite, but perfect."

"I can find something else."

Brian laughed. "You're worrying about nothing. You'll go, take the pie with you, and I'll end up coming to find you because you won't want to come home. Okay, maybe not. You go and get changed while I make my sandwich. I'll dig out the pie so it can be defrosting. Don't be surprised if there's a piece miss– It's okay, I'm only joking, although if there is some left…"

"Then I'll bring a piece home with me."

"Deal."

So Odelle went upstairs, put on her 'anniversary' dress; a delightful floor-length red number with intricate birds of paradise embroidered into the heavy silk.

She walked into the kitchen as Brian was putting his sandwich into a clear food bag. The pie lay on a plate by the kettle.

"I can't wear this," Odelle said, as he opened his mouth to speak.

"I'd forgotten how beautiful you look in that."

"But it's too much."

"Maybe you're right."

"Oh, Brian."

"You'll be the belle of the ball, that's for sure. Make an impression."

He put his sandwich into his rucksack, walked over to his wife, took her hand, palm-down like an old-fashioned royal, and kissed it. "Okay now?"

She nodded.

"Excellent. Well, I'm ready too so why don't I walk you there?"

"Brian, it's three doors down."

"We can't have you looking like that with no escort, even if it is for five seconds. Besides, with the pie and a bottle of wine, how are you going to ring the bell?"

"I don't think they have one."

"Knock, then."

"You do have a point."

"Exactly. I'll get the wine, you get the pie, I've put it on a plate."

"Are you sure I shouldn't get changed?"

"No, love, you look fabulous. A knockout."

She blushed, a shade lighter than her dress.

Brian locked the door then followed Odelle to number seventeen. She still looked nervous as she approached the front door. From the noise inside, it was evident that the party was already in full swing.

As she was about to knock, a grinning Roger opened the door. "Brian! Odelle! I'm so glad you could make it. Do come in and meet my temporary houseguest."

"Brian can't stay, I'm afraid, Roger," Odelle said. "He's been called into work but…" She stopped talking as a tall tanned svelte figure walked down the hall towards her.

Brian, anticipating his wife's reaction, handed Roger the bottle of wine and Banoffee pie then smiled as she screamed and rushed forward to hug her sister.

## Court (A Shaggy Dog Story)

Gerry had never been to court before. He'd seen it plenty of times on TV but it was different in real life. Bigger, noisier, scarier. Having watched most of the detective dramas his Sky+ memory bank could handle, he knew the language, the instructions that were passed around the room, but even being there for the prosecution made him nervous.

He was early. He knew that. Far too early. It would be hours before he'd be called in. Less than that before the case started but he figured he'd probably have to stay in the corridor until then, on the hard wooden bench.

Maybe he'd stagger the coffee runs. One every half hour… or every hour. If he could last that long. But then he shouldn't drink much in case he was in the toilet when they called his name. That would be unlucky. But he could be quick.

Even the solicitor wasn't there yet. He'd met her once, at her office, coincidentally round the corner from his. 'Finance Manager' the sign on the door read. His, that is, not hers.

He'd not really wanted to get involved but being the only person to see what had happened, he'd not really had any choice. He'd been the one to call the police, the paramedics, the fire brigade. Waited until they'd arrived. Let them take a statement. The police. Given them his name.

And he was the one feeling guilty. He hadn't done anything wrong. He'd just been cycling past the tennis court on his way home, a bit earlier than usual but it had been a nice day so he'd treated himself to an early finish. He was a manager; no one queries last-thing appointments when you're a manager.

So it was the wrong place at the wrong time. And he hadn't really been paying attention, only you expect people to be playing tennis on a tennis court, don't you? You don't expect…. that. And it wasn't even dark. Not close to it. Four o'clock on a June weekday. Six hours before it gets dark.

Gerry reckoned it had been a dare. On reflection, the woman hadn't seemed that bothered. The guy looked less pleased but then he'd been in too much pain to say anything. That would beat carpet burns any day.

Gerry wasn't sure where the frying pan came into it. Figured the gravel would have caused enough friction without adding

Teflon to the mixture. Gerry laughed at the omelette-type pun and watched a nervous young woman in a suit scuttle by. Not the same woman from the tennis court, Gerry didn't think she'd be nervous of anything, but a small shrew-like thing heading towards the courthouse ground floor ladies toilet.

It was the dog that Gerry felt sorry for. Tied up in the corner, attached to the green plastic-coated metal fencing, having to watch… what Gerry ended up watching.

He had to admire how nimble they were. He'd read snippets of the Karma Sutra and didn't remember seeing a picture for the position they'd got themselves into. Didn't leave much to the imagination either but then he'd had to admire theirs.

And to be doing all that while wearing see-through cut-out wet suits. Gerry didn't even know they existed but thought it might make his next trip to Blue Corner Wall in Palau a bit more interesting.

The paramedics hadn't seemed that surprised. Gerry thought he'd heard one of them call the woman by name… Sindy, Candy, something ending in 'dee'. He laughed again and thought of Sandra Dee and how she'd gone from sweet to sexy in an hour and a half. Or however long Grease ran for.

Gerry couldn't imagine the woman at the tennis court ever being sweet, although whatever the toffee-coloured goo was they were rubbing over each other may have helped.

Gerry was debating another trip to the coffee machine when he sensed someone standing over him. He looked up and recognised the dark blonde bob and pale pink lipstick of his solicitor.

"Hello, Mr Walker," she said, with the broadest whitest smile Gerry had ever seen. "Shall we go and have some fun?"

## An American Werewolf In London

"Brian."

"Sorry?"

"The name's Brian… Latham."

"Oh, hi. Donald Varda."

"Canadian?"

"American. Do I sound Canadian?"

"To be honest, I don't know the difference. It's like Australia and New Zealand but if you call Kiwis Ozzies they don't like it. The same for– "

"Kiwis? Ozzies?"

"New Zealanders. Australians."

"Oh, okay. And what do you call us?"

"Yanks."

"Yeah, that's right. So what are 'Poms'?"

"That's what Australians call us. Can't remember why now."

"I didn't think people talked to each other on trains but I guess you Brits are more open than we give you credit for. We don't in the States."

"It's a shame, isn't it? Even just a few stops, it's worth saying something."

"Sure."

"I see a lot of the same people in here every morning, every evening, and they never talk. Who knows what they might have in common. So, are you in London on business or pleasure, Donald?"

"A bit of both."

"That's nice. What do you do?"

"I'm a werewolf."

"Pardon me?"

"A werewolf."

"I thought that's what you said. You, er… make a living out of being a, er… werewolf?"

"Not as much as you'd think."

"It's not something I've ever thought about. You're the first one I've met… This is for a play or something, right?"

"Of course. My god, you didn't think I actually am a werewolf!"

"You do look the part, I have to say. I've never seen eyes quite like yours and you've even got eyebrows that meet in the middle."

"They're real."

"Wow. So you were born for that part then really, weren't you?"

"You could say that."

"Tottenham Court Road. This is my stop."

"Mine too. You in the theatre, Brian?"

"No. I'm an accountant. My office is at the top of Grape Street, just off Shaftesbury Avenue. Do you know it?"

"No, sorry."

"It's a fairly small road. You probably wouldn't have noticed it, unless you're Cuban."

"Why Cuban?"

"Their Embassy's there, at the other end of the road. We do accounts for a couple of the theatres but no, just a desk job, nothing half as exciting as being on stage, performing in front of all those people. I used to meet people. I sold hoovers. You know, vacuum cleaners."

"Oh, yeah."

"Just part-time, while I was studying. Before that I was a catering assistant but I love numbers so ended up doing what I do now. It's funny what fate has in store, isn't it?"

"It is, indeed."

"The ticket goes face up, with the strip… that's it."

"Thanks."

"So how long are you here for?"

"I don't really know. I'm just going to see what happens. If everyone's as friendly as you, I think I'll stay a while."

"That's nice. I've lived in London all my life, wouldn't want to leave. There's a guy at work who's from America. California, I think. Can't understand why he'd swap the sun for rainy old London. Actually it's not as wet as everybody thinks."

"It's been nice so far."

"You've picked the best time; July, August. Busy time for your show as well, I guess, lots of tourists wanting to see the sights. Everyone goes to the theatre when they're in London."

"I'm hoping so."

"Okay, this is me, top of Grape Street. Just down there. Red door on the right. See it? Oh. Sure I'll show you. If you keep going to the end and turn right, Shaftesbury Avenue is the next right. I don't remember seeing your play being advertised anywhere. Working where I do, I can't usually escape the posters."

"We're doing rehearsals at the moment. Won't be out for a while."

"Here we are then. Well, Donald, it's been great chatting with you. I hope your play, and stay, go well. I might see if I can pop along. You know, once it airs, so to speak."

"I'm not sure there are any tickets left."

"Really? I thought you said… Never mind. Maybe next time. I'll look out for you."

"I'm not hard to miss."

"No, and… oh look, you've even got the teeth."

"I have."

"They are rather magnificent. Erm… What are you… Donald? What? No!"

## Furry Like A Dog

Sydney was a little grey bear with a bright red bow around his neck. He was very handsome but quite shy. He'd been bought as an Easter present for Darcy Hutton and they went everywhere together. Darcy's bike had a basket on the front and wherever the family's cycle rides took them, Sydney would be there, leading the way.

As winter approached, the weather got colder and they went out less.

One Friday evening, Sydney was sitting above the fireplace in the lounge. Darcy had gone to bed without him which was unusual, but Sydney didn't mind because he would be there to greet him in the morning.

As Sydney sat against a carriage clock, he watched Darcy's father putting together a big wooden thing. Mrs Hutton was busy in the kitchen and the lovely smells made Sydney hungry. It was a very cold evening and the fire was so warm that he soon fell asleep.

The next day, Sydney woke to find the household rushing around, too busy to pay any attention to him. It took him a minute to realise what was happening. It was Darcy's seventh birthday. Sydney had heard Mr and Mrs Hutton talking about it earlier in the week.

Darcy was begging his parents to let him open his presents and they finally gave in. Sydney watched as streams of wrapping paper produced a plane model kit, a new cycle helmet and computer games. Sydney was grateful there weren't any toys like him to take his place.

As Darcy's father wheeled the final present into the lounge, Sydney recognised it as the wooden box. The back was plain but when it was turned round the front was covered with wire mesh and inside he could see something moving. Darcy gasped then clapped his hands wildly.

Sydney was too far away to see what all the excitement was about and wondered what kind of thing could live in there. Maybe it was a dog. One of Darcy's friends had a dog but he didn't live in anything like this.

He watched Darcy open the door. There wasn't just one thing in there but two. They were furry like a dog, but much smaller. Darcy leant forward and picked one of them out. It was grey, like Sydney, and was very handsome. For the first time in his life, Sydney was jealous. Darcy frowned and looked up at his mum.

"They're guinea pigs, Darcy," she explained.

"Guinea pigs!" Darcy cheered as he dug back into the cage for the other furball. This one was completely white with pink eyes.

*A funny looking thing*, Sydney thought, *not handsome at all*.

*Pigs*? he then wondered. The only pigs he'd seen before were on a cycle ride to Mr Parker's farm where Darcy fed them. Whatever type of pig they were, Sydney felt happy they wouldn't eat him.

Sydney watched as Darcy struggled to hold both of them.

Darcy's mother took the white one. "They are very special guinea pigs, Darcy," she said. "Auntie Lily has sent them all the way from Scotland for you. The grey one is a type called 'Cinnamonrex' and the white one is an 'Ivorysatin'. They're both boys so we have to be very careful they don't fight.

"Don't worry, Mum." Darcy beamed. "I will stay with them *all* the time." He looked the guinea pig in his hands. "I'll call this one Lewis." He then looked at white one which was wriggling in his mother's hands. "And that one, Duncan." Darcy's mum smiled as she knew her sister would be delighted that Darcy had named them after his slightly older cousins.

Sydney started to feel sad. What Darcy said about looking after his new pets meant that he wouldn't have time for him anymore.

Darcy turned away from the cage and looked around the room until he spotted his best friend. "Look, Sydney!" Darcy said as he walked towards him, still with Lewis in his hands. "We've got some new friends. We can't take them with us on the bike but we can play together in the house, wouldn't that be fun?"

*Yes*, Sydney thought, *that WOULD be fun*.

## Bill The Bag Man

They say everyone has someone, but there are those few who slip the radar, made someone their everything then lost them, moved area for a fresh start.

Bill's wife Kitty had been the one interested in shopping, he'd just sit reading the sports section until she either bought (usually) or moved on to another shop (or both).

She'd been the one with the good job. He'd never understood what a gorgeous sales executive had seen in a binman like Bill but he made her laugh, they made each other laugh, and when they were told they couldn't have children, it didn't seem to matter. They used the money a buggy would have cost to go away for the weekend, cot money paid for a London show.

Whenever she bought a new suit she'd call it an investment, but to Bill it looked the same as the one she'd been wearing the day before. "Quality over quantity," she'd say and she seemed to have both but it was her money and it made her happy, so Bill had no complaints.

"We should do a car boot sale," he'd suggested, but then agreed when she'd said they'd only get a fraction of the money back and that she still wore or used everything she'd bought, so he'd nodded again.

But then she started buying smaller sizes, seemed paler each shopping trip and when she'd collapsed, he'd wanted to cry at how light she felt lifting her in the car.

As she got thinner, the trips increased; she'd wanted to explore while she could, then her mode of transport changed from the London Underground to a wheelchair by the sea front.

Finally, shopping was all she enjoyed but she'd buy things for him, saying she had more than enough to last a lifetime. Bill knew she meant hers.

He'd not wanted all the clutter around the house before but when she'd died, he begun to see its attraction; it kept him company. Inanimate objects they may have been, but every now and then he'd get out a bag and look at the contents; smiling if it was something he'd bought, crying if it was hers.

So he kept up the tradition, went in every shop with a 'sale' sign then bought regardless of whether reduced or not, adding it to the pile when he got home.

He started having to step over things, cupboard space a premium, but it felt like exercise. He'd become practiced at making mounds that stayed upright despite resembling the leaning Tower of Pisa.

They incorporated tunnels and he felt like his childhood guinea pigs nestling through straw. He'd even chirruped and laughed. He wasn't sure how Kitty would have felt about his existence but he knew she wouldn't have wanted him mourning and having all her things around him was soothing.

Routines kept him sane; Tesco Monday afternoons, picking a different assistant each time, the library Wednesday mornings where self-service meant he could be a no one. Friday lunchtimes were foil-wrapped sandwiches in the park with a bottle of orange juice on a warm day or flask of tea when cold.

He began thinking that retirement wasn't as bad as people made out and he'd pop into the pound shop on the way home, filling a couple of carrier bags with anything bright and cheerful; toys for grandchildren he'd never have, squeaky bones for a dog long gone, short-date shortbread from a Scottish loch. He'd have them with his cup of tea so he treated himself to the local paper from Mr Patel's.

Pulling out the shortbread, he started a new layer of bags in one corner of the lounge. He'd put the kettle on and stretch his legs in the garden then work his way back to his favourite chair to see what the outside world had been up to, according to the Holford Gazette.

The kettle was boiling when he remembered he'd left his mug by the chair and nestled his way, knowing every square inch of carpet. He'd just turned round, mug in hand, when his foot kicked a bag and he heard plastic shifting. It was his back that felt the blow first, then his hip, his shoulder, his head.

As Bill took his last breath, he saw Kitty's face and he knew everything was going to be okay.

## Plenty More Fish

"Plenty more fish in the sea."

You know you'll lose your temper if she says that one more time, but you nod, not looking up from the magazine you're reading, and change the subject. Kai's the reason why you're back living with your mother, and you don't want to be reminded of either. "Nell said there might be a job going at Al Fresco."

"You're going to be a waitress?"

"Better than nothing, Mum."

"It's a start, I suppose."

You loved being a waitress while you were at university and it doesn't faze you to do it again – you've never been afraid of hard work – but…

"Of course, your father would have wanted better for you."

He would, and it does make life easier that he's no longer around, but out of the two of them, you know it's him you'd rather have standing by the kitchen sink drying the dishes you washed.

"Maybe you'll meet someone new there."

Not quite 'plenty more fish' but it grates all the same. Everything about her grates but you can't afford a B&B and don't want to impose on friends, so you pull your weight and muddle along, spending as much time with Nell as you can.

Her name flashes up on your phone. "Hiya."

"Hi. I've spoken to Max."

"Cool. And?"

"He said come in at six and he'll give you a trial run."

"What?"

"Six. Trial run."

"What about an interview? Doesn't he even want to see my CV?"

"Hold on." Nell covers the phone for a few seconds. "He says bring it, but it's only a piece of paper. Said it's all about ability and personality. Don't drop anything, impress the customers, impress him, and the job's yours."

"Just like that?"

"Just like that. He's not a red tape guy. Gotta go. See you at six."

"See you… and thanks."

"No problem. Will be great to see more of you."

You press the red icon, and clutch the phone.

"Good news?" the voice over your shoulder asks.

Without turning round, you reply. "Yes, I have to be there at six."

"Good," she says, and disappears upstairs.

You stick out your tongue then smile. This is the best news you've had in a while. You've never met Max but figure that if Nell can handle him then he can't be too bad.

The only Maxs you know are off the TV; the chauffeur from Hart to Hart, and Bradley's father on Eastenders.

You never knew what Tanya saw in him, but then you can say that about you and Kai now. Easy to think in hindsight. A college crush gone serious then gone wrong. The teacher/student relationship that rarely works.

Nell beams. "You look great!"

You look down at your plain white shirt, black skirt, black thick tights and comfy black shoes. You want to say "This old thing?" but you'd cut the labels off less than an hour before. "Thanks, Nell."

"Okay. Come on. Let's introduce you to the great man."

You take a deep breath as you follow her through the double-swing kitchen doors. Releasing your breath comes out as a cough as Max holds out his hand. He's a little older than you, nearer Bradley's dad than the chauffeur, but much better looking and a confident, rather than sleazy, smile.

"Sorry," you say, wiping your palm on your skirt and hold out your hand.

He laughs and shakes it. "You've seen Gordon Ramsay on TV?"

You nod, slowly lowering your hand as Max releases it.

"He's a pussy cat compared with me."

You go to say something about how you've always thought him not that bad, but Max continues. "Only joking. I do expect you to work hard but we play hard too. Have a laugh and a joke by all means but not out there." He points towards the restaurant's seating area. "Six to midnight, Thursday to Saturday and Monday. Tuesday lunchtimes ten 'til four. Wednesday and Sunday off. Okay?"

"Okay, but..."

"But?"

"You've not seen me work yet."

Max laughs. "Not here, sure, but you worked at Tantés, didn't you?"

"Yes. Yes, I did. How…?" Then it dawns on you that you have seen him before, served him before. You look at Nell and blush.

## Hold On

No one's told him how he should be feeling but it's nice… a kind of tingling.

He stares at his new neighbour. He wants to curl his mouth, if he had one, like he's seen those pink stick things do. He thinks they're called 'peeple'. He's heard one of them say "sum peeple!" but he can't be sure. He has to call them something and they're small, like beetles, so they're the beetle peeple.

He doesn't understand their language, still feels like he doesn't belong, even after all these years.

He did once, he thought, hear familiar words, his mother tongue, but it came from a little black box. He was listening hard until one of the peeple prodded the box and it crackled, like it was in pain, then the voice was replaced by music… loud, unpleasant, not like the birds. He knows music from the birds but that doesn't help because he can't speak their language either.

The new neighbour's really quiet. He's sure he should be picking up something… maybe she's still too young. He can't remember how old he was when he first started sensing things… not feeling, he doesn't feel as such, but he's old, wise, and knows how life goes – in his part of it anyway.

He's seen thousands of peeple coming and going, using him as shade, shelter, protection… a climbing frame, until one got very high then screamed as it… 'he' went down very quickly. A moving white box with coloured lights came and put him, and a screaming bigger 'she', inside and went away, making lots of noise.

He prefers it when it's quiet, and dark, it's cooler when it's dark. Sometimes it gets too hot. He thinks where he's from, originally, is colder, except he can't really remember. He remembers a journey, going over some water but most of it was land, green like here.

He thinks he was young, like his neighbour, when he arrived. It was a long time ago. When she's old enough, he'll ask her if she remembers. There won't be so far back for her to think.

After the white box went, some more peeple came and put a barrier around him, and big yellow squares with black squiggles he couldn't understand but he knew what it meant; that no one could touch him anymore, couldn't climb, couldn't hug.

He liked it when peeple touched him, even when they cut squiggles into him. It didn't hurt, just tickled a little, felt nice, like they were making him their own, like he belonged.

But now he has a different kind of company, his own kind and he can't wait for her to grow, to have someone to 'feel' with.

There's that tingling again. It's like… no, it can't be. He tells himself not to be so silly. He knows 'silly' from the little peeple. They'd do funny things with their faces then tell each other not to be silly, but silly looks like a lot of fun.

It is! It… no, it can't be… It is! A new bud!

He'd felt sick for ages, not like the little 'he' who'd fallen from him because 'he' hadn't moved… but tired, old. It's not like that now. It feels like when little 'he' started climbing, to explore, reach out… grow.

They're taking the barrier away! He must be better. He can have peeple touch him again. He feels like being very silly today!

There's a big 'he' with a large shiny stick. What's he doing? He's pulling a bit of… something out of it and it's making a roaring noise, like he'd seen one of the little 'he's do which made a little 'she' scream.

All the other peeple laughed but he didn't find it funny. The little 'she' had looked scared. He remembered scared from when the sky grew dark, and the rain came, and there were loud noises way above them and the peeple screamed and ran to him, and he made them feel safe.

Hey! The big 'he' is cutting squiggles into him, making him his own. It's not unpleasant but it's not stopping, he must really like him.

He feels all wobbly, wants to put his branches out to balance himself. He felt like this when he got sick, but he doesn't feel sick now, he feels… free. He feels… aliv…

"Timber!"

"Hold on!"

## The Lake At Dusk

As Jemma walked through the front door, she felt like she'd been through a washing machine only someone had forgotten to set it to spin.

"Stay there!" her mother shouted from the kitchen doorway when she saw the state of her. "I don't want you dripping through the house."

"But Mum, I'm freezing."

"The heating's on, you'll soon dry."

Jemma went to step towards the radiator.

"Don't!"

"But..."

"No."

"Can't I at least...?" Jemma looked down at her shoes.

"Alright then," her mother conceded. "But just your shoes. You and they stay on the mat."

Jemma was used to being spoken to like this but she thought even this was harsh.

"Where have you been anyway?"

This was different; curiosity bordering on concern, a flicker of compassion. "The shopping centre," Jemma lied.

"No you haven't. They shut at seven on a Friday."

Jemma said nothing.

"Well?"

Jemma knew she'd find out eventually. "The woods."

Her mother shrugged, truth clearly outweighing risk.

"And it was scary," Jemma whispered.

"You're dripping," her mother grumbled, throwing the washing-up towel she'd been holding. Despite falling short of its intended target, she ignored it and returned to the kitchen, getting another tea towel from a drawer and continuing to dry the dishes from the evening meal Jemma had missed.

The smell of the food still clung to the air making Jemma's stomach growl. She stared at the towel then at the kitchen. Shaking her body like a dog, she figured she'd be dry enough to tread the few yards in socked feet to retrieve the towel but putting her right foot forward, she heard a squelch, so bent down to take off her socks. Like a gymnast she leaned towards the radiator and hung them over the top of the curved white metal; the metal that was piping hot; the heat that would suck up her moisture if only it was allowed to.

"What you doing?"

Jemma looked round to see her brother, Leyton, standing in the lounge doorway holding a yoghurt pot and licking the spoon.

"Trying to get warm. What does it look like?"

"You look stupid."

"Thanks. Charming as ever."

"You been seeing Logan again?"

"How do you know his name?"

"Everyone at school's talking about it. The romance of the year."

"Hardly."

"Why? He dumped you?"

"No!"

"He has!"

"Shut up!"

"Did he tell you to meet him by the lake at dusk, all romantic like?"

"What?"

"He did the same to Georgia, only he didn't turn up then told everyone at school the next day that she was easy, just by her being there."

"Georgia? My Georgia?"

"Yes, your Georgia. Bezzie mate Georgia."

"When?"

"Last week sometime. When you was…"

"Were."

"Yeah, whatever."

"When I was visiting Nan in hospital?"

"Yeah, that was it."

"Georgia phoned me. Crying. Said her uncle had died. I didn't even know she had one."

"Probably doesn't. Just wanted you to feel sorry for her. So you went through Priory Woods, to meet him and he didn't–"

"Change the record, Ley."

"What?"

"Record. Round flat thing made of black plastic… oh, never mind."

“And you went in the dark. Even you’re not that stupid.”

“It wasn’t dark.”

“Not when you went, no, but… You waited that long? You are that stu–”

“I wasn’t waiting.”

He looked down then picked up the tea towel. “You want this?”

Jemma nodded.

“Okay,” Leyton said, handing it out to her, just short of reach.

Jemma closed her eyes and sighed. Leyton stepped nearer and nudged her hand with it. “Here. I’m not that mean. Not like–”

Jemma’s eyes sprung open then glared at her brother.

“Alright,” he said, “subject closed.”

They stared at each other until he spoke again. “Was it really horrible?”

“Please don’t.”

“I don’t mean being stood up, though I bet that was… Okay. No, I mean going through the wood after dark. It’s supposed to be haunted.”

“Now you tell me.”

“You didn’t exactly ask. Didn’t tell anyone you were going, did you?”

Jemma shook her head.

“What was it like?” Leyton continued.

“Quiet. No birds, nothing. Like death.”

“Who are you talking to?” Jemma’s mother asked as she walked through the hall to take her husband a cup of tea.

“No one, Mum,” she said.

Her mother paused. “Jemma… please don’t go down there again. You know how I feel about that place. Leyton made that mistake. We can’t lose you too. Okay?”

“Okay, Mum,” Jemma said, feeling warmer than she had in a long time, and even managed a smile.

## Beyond The Blue Horizon

Tel stared out through the treble-layer glass at the blue horizon. It seemed to be growing a shade darker every day but he looked down at the printer, at the reports, and they didn't show anything out of the ordinary; the heartbeat lines pulsating in rhythm with no hint of a deviation. If there was an attack due the machine wasn't sensing it.

There was only one other explanation Tel knew, or rather had heard of. It had never happened in his lifetime.

It was going to rain.

He couldn't say anything. They'd laugh at him.

No one knew what effect real water would have on man-made water. Would they just blend or would one substance react with the other? Kill the other?

Maybe this was the attack after all. They, the powers that be, had said it was to be an air attack. *Could it be something as simple as rain?*

"Rain?" an alarmed voice said behind him.

Tel swung round. "Stop doing that!"

"What?" Farbe looked innocent.

"Sneak up on me… read my mind."

*I only read the good bits*, Farbe said not moving his mouth. "Now what's this about rain? You know we haven't had that since–"

"And we won't," Tel interrupted. "The reports are fine, everything's fine." He gave a nervous chuckle.

"Then why is the sky getting darker, bluer?"

Tel turned to look at it. "You've noticed it too?"

"No." Farbe leaned in. "I was listening to you."

Tel stepped backwards, standing, not by accident, on Farbe's foot.

"Ow!"

Tel faced his colleague. "How long have you been standing there?"

"Since just after you were thinking about what you'd like to do to Evetha." Farbe grinned.

"Before…? Before! How?"

"I'm a Mark IV, remember." He tapped the side of his white metal-clad head. "Improved sensors." He then shook his foot to clear the pain, which appeared to do the trick. "Right," he said, as if taking authority. "What are we going to do about this rain?"

Tel shrugged.

"There's a contingency plan somewhere, isn't there?"

Tel's eyes lit up. He opened a drawer under one of the desks and pulled out a red file.

Farbe stepped forward to join him.

Turning to the index, Tel ran his finger down the alphabetical list then read out, "Railway incidents… Raised blood pressure… Raisins stuck in throat." He looked over at Farbe. "Raisins? They've got raisins but nothing about rain? What are we supposed to do?"

"Maybe you're wrong."

"I don't think so. I can feel it in my…"

"Water?" Farbe laughed.

"Bones. I've just got this horrible feeling…"

"Then you should tell someone."

"They won't believe me."

"I believe you."

"No, you don't."

Farbe put on his sincere expression. "I do."

"Then you tell them."

"Oh, I can't do that. I'm only a Mark IV."

"What were you saying about improved…?"

"Sensors. But we're still young. No Mark IV I know of has got past Assistant, and I'm not even there yet." He hesitated then thrust a finger in the air. "I know!"

"Yes?"

"Let's ask a Mark V!"

"What? There are no Mark Vs."

"Yes there are. There's one. It was in the paper." Farbe held up his right hand, palm facing Tel, and a screen within it burst into life.

Tel read the first few lines then looked back at Farbe. "That's no good. We don't know where it is."

Farbe sighed. “If you’d read a bit further you’d have got to the bit saying where it was going to be delivered.”

Tel looked out the window, to the right of the horizon, to the city complex and the thousands of home-pods. “Go on, where.”

“Here.”

Tel turned to Farbe. “Here? Really? When?”

Before Farbe could reply, an electronic swish sounded behind them and a door slid open. It was the same sound as they used on the first Star Trek TV series, Tel’s boss being a big fan, had been insistent on it.

They stood there open-mouthed as a gold version of Farbe glided in. “Hello, I’m New.”

“We know,” Farbe said first.

“No, my name is New.”

“Oh,” Tel said. “And erm… what do you do?”

“Everything,” New replied, his voice changing tone with every word, like a gentle stream on a summer’s day.

“Everything?” Tel repeated.

“He does,” Farbe said, looking at Tel, then scrolling down the text on his palm screen. “He even tells the future.” Farbe turned back to face New. “We have a question for you.”

“I know,” New said.

“Of course,” Farbe laughed. “You can tell the future.”

“Rain,” Tel butted in.

New faced Tel and gulped.

## In The Stars

Roxy clicks on the left mouse button dragging the 'Table' option to three columns by thirteen rows. She lets go and a chart appears before her. In the first row she types 'Months', 'Signs' and 'Scenarios'.

In the left column she slots in 'January' to 'December', then in the middle, she types the names of the symbols sitting on the die in front of her, just as she sees them, thrown at random: moon, shooting star, torch, clock, arrow (pointing south west), magnifying glass, eye, castle, fish, flower, bat and sheep.

Pausing at June, her month, she laughs and types 'magnifying glass'. "Time to buy new glasses," she says, squinting at the screen.

With the second column full, she starts on the third, looks at the empty space next to 'January' and 'moon', then closes her eyes. Tilting back her head, she waits for inspiration. "Moon... circle." Then it comes to her. 'One aspect of your life will come full circle. Rather than thinking you're working backwards, embrace it.'

February's shooting star prompts her to type, 'With determination you can achieve a lot. Grasp every opportunity with both hands however small it may seem at the time.'

Someone born in March could expect to 'be a shining light in the life of someone who's feeling low and needs their spirits lifted'. "Grasp, embrace, spirits lifting," she says out loud then laughs, "I could do with someone to grasp and embrace me; that would definitely lift my spirits."

April's clock prompt advises its recipients to 'use their time more wisely' whereas May's arrow suggests that he or she should 'consider taking an alternate path if they were unhappy with the choices they were making'.

At June's 'new glasses' she types 'You will start to see things more clearly' then settles on 'keep an eye on your finances' for July followed by 'home improvements' for August and 'an exotic holiday perhaps travelling by sea' for September.

'Flower' she finds quite easy, steering the October-born reader to 'surprise a loved one with an impromptu gift such as flowers or chocolates'. 'Bat' and 'sheep' are initially more difficult, but she finally settles on 'try a new sport' and 'resist the temptation to follow the flock today, break away and do something daring'.

She copies and pastes the details into an email, gives it one more read, tweaks a word here and there, then presses 'send' and imagines it winging its way across the ether to the online magazine's editor for publication overnight.

Remembering June's prompt, Roxy rings her local opticians and is given a cancellation slot for the next morning.

As she walks to the town centre the next day, she thinks about the descriptions and wonders, feeling like a fortune teller, whether she should have been a bit more upbeat, telling people what they want to hear.

"Oh well, too late," she says, pulling the heavy glass doors of the opticians.

"Oh dear," a voice says behind her and Roxy turns round.

"Sorry?" she says, to the tall man looming over her.

"You say you're late? They don't like you being late here."

"No, not late. I was referring to…" It's then that Roxy spots his dog collar. She's not sure what it is about vicars but they make her feel a little uneasy. Ever since she'd watched the Omen movies, churches had never felt the same.

They report their names to the reception and are pointed towards two green chairs.

"Sorry, my mistake," he says to Roxy. "I shouldn't eavesdrop. Dreadful habit. Got me into trouble before. You think I'd learn my lesson but listening is… hazard of the job I suppose."

Roxy laughs then wonders if she should. *He's not God himself*, she thinks. *He's human too.* Then she notices he's fiddling with the collar as if it's too tight. She raises her eyebrows and he looks down at his hand.

"I've been doing that for days. Like it doesn't fit anymore."

"It looks alright to me," she lies, but then feels guilty. She's never understood the relevance of the white strip of material but then no one's taken the time to explain it to her. He, on the other hand, looks the patient type; sitting next to an ill parishioner for hours on end, waiting for a confessioner to work through a list.

"I don't normally," he interrupts her thoughts, "but I read my stars today. December. It said I should 'leave the flock, break away and do something daring' and I don't normally believe them but..."

*That's funny*, she thinks, *nor do I, but something tells me maybe I should.*

## Best In Show

'Best in Show three times' the advert read. 'Genuine reason for sale.'

Hester was delighted at the perfectly-behaved five-year-old tan and white Shih Tzu.

Cassius Princeton Tuffnell III looked the part, acted it, even held its own head and tail up, as if she were a judge and thirty-two Bernett Close the Crufts Show ring.

"Is that the best price?" Hester asked, holding up the advert.

The man nodded. "You can't put a figure on breeding."

"No, I suppose you can't," Hester conceded, and counted the bundle of twenty-pound notes into the man's large rough hands. They, and he, looked as if they'd been in this profession for years, the rosettes and trophies gleaming behind a tall glass-doored cabinet.

"He comes with a certificate of course," the man added, as the last twenty-pound note touched the top of the stack.

Hester smiled and watched the man close his hands reverently as if the money meant more to him than the dog.

Cassius III was sitting on a red velvet-cushioned chair placed between the couple and looked at one then the other as if watching from the royal box at Wimbledon.

As the man folded the notes in half and stuffed them into his khaki trouser pocket, the dog fixed his gaze on Hester as if he'd known the transaction's significance and that he was now hers.

"So he's good in the car?" Hester asked.

"Aye. Used to it."

"Of course." Hester stared at the colourful cabinet on the opposite wall. She went to step nearer, but the man spoke again, distracting her.

"Have you brought a cage?"

"Erm, no. Just a harness. Will that be alright?"

"S'pose." The man walked into the hall, to a small table. He handed her the certificate. "Are you going to show him too? He still has plenty of years left in him."

The dog looked up at the man when he spoke then tilted its head on one side.

The man opened the front door for Hester and as she passed, he held out his hand which she shook. “Pleasure doing business with you,” he beamed, showing a gold tooth with a ruby inset that Hester thought hideous.

He slammed the door before she’d reached her car.

She harnessed Cassius, gave him a rub under his chin and drove away.

Mistress and dog made eye contact in the rear view mirror. “Best in show, hey?” Hester said half-statement, half-question.

The dog shook its head.

“Do you understand me?”

Cassius nodded.

“Wow, you are clever.”

“You don’t know the half of it,” the dog replied, making Hester swerve, almost crashing into an oncoming taxi.

She pulled into the kerb, switched off the engine, released her seatbelt and turned round. “You can talk?”

“Sure.”

“And he knew that?”

“Of course not. You saw him, he’s a heathen. Plenty of years left, the cheek!”

“But… wow!”

“I know.” Cassius laughed.

“You can talk!” Hester repeated.

“You’ll get used to it.”

“The newspapers will–”

“They won’t. I don’t talk to newspapers. I’m not a commodity. I have feelings. Like when you asked for a discount. It was a bit–”

“I’m sorry about that.”

“It’s okay. I probably would have done the same. It was a lot of money. You can call me Cass, by the way, none of that Cassius III rubbish. I’m not royalty.”

“But the certificate…”

“Fake, just like all those rosettes and trophies.”

“Were you not best in show?”

“Once or twice but small stuff; village fetes. Never Crufts and the likes.”

“Where did he get them all?”

"eBay. That's why he wouldn't let you near them."

"That figures. Are you stolen?"

"Oh, no. He won me in a bet. Still think I'm worth it?"

"Absolutely."

"Thought so. You're obviously a dog lover."

"I am, but what makes you say that?"

"Because you went for the chin rather than a pat on the head. I hate that. So demeaning. So, are you going to show me?"

"I hadn't planned to."

"Thank God for that. I'm not religious, by the way, it's just a saying."

Hester nodded.

"I love travelling," Cass continued, "going to new places, meeting new people. It's all that preening and prodding. You know."

Hester had watched every Crufts over the past twenty years but had recently become disillusioned with it. She'd seen buying Cass as rescuing him. "I do."

"So what's the plan?"

"No plan really. Just hang out together."

"Sounds good to me."

Hester looked at the dashboard clock. "It's not even lunchtime yet. Fancy a trip to the Peaks?"

Cass barked and wagged his tail.

"I'll take that as a 'yes' then," Hester said, refastening her seatbelt.

## Quiet And Noisy

The candle flickered while the man crouched over my right ankle. It looked like a candle but I think it was probably a lighter.

Someone had put their briefcase under my head and I could feel the catch digging in. I didn't like to complain because it meant I had a better view of the man. Compared to the pain in my leg, my head was okay. Uncomfortable, not painful really.

Pain's good though isn't it because it means I can feel it, that it's going to be okay. I know there's something on it, my leg, pressing down, so once they get it off they can move me, take me to hospital.

I remember shouting when I first came to, but no one took any notice apart from that one guy and it seemed like I was the only one making any noise, so I stopped. The woman next to me had taken the full force of the metal caving in and I think died instantly because she didn't answer me, and she hadn't stopped talking since she'd got on at Milton Keynes, so I know she would have said something if she could have done.

The lights going out was the worst thing. I hate the dark.

Noise. I had expected there to be more noise but I remember the impact then the quiet. Too quiet. I thought everyone was dead but then I sensed people moving around, shadows, then the pain of my leg took over.

I think the man went to tend to someone else, there are bound to be people worse off than me, but the briefcase is still there.

My head's beginning to hurt a bit now and if I concentrate on that, my ankle isn't so painful. I know I should think of something else, good things, like meeting Melissa for lunch.

Oh shit, I must phone her, tell her what's happened, that I'm okay. She'll hear it on the news and worry. She's a worrier when everything's going well, so…

A light! There's a light! Hello? Over here! No, this way…

It's okay. I'll wait. I'm not going anywhere and the train certainly isn't. Not for a while at least. They'll have to clear it out the way, bring in cranes. The poor sods on the later commutes are going to be pretty pissed off. They'll either have to divert… not sure if they can do that.

Buses. They put on extra buses, don't they?

Something doesn't smell very nice. Not like petrol or diesel so that's good. At least we're not going to blow up.

And it's cold. Whatever ran into us… it definitely ran into us because it came into the side, we didn't run into it, must have made a hole… of course it did, you stupid sod. Even if it caved the side in there'll be a hole.

Poor train company. I don't usually feel sorry for them… costs me over a grand a year just to get to work and back, but trains are expensive aren't they. I suppose they'll have insurance.

It's still quiet. Can't understand why there aren't people panicking, you know, pulling at things, trying to get out or get other people out. I know someone will come for me… back for me soon. They know I'm alive so they'll come.

Just need to get to my bag. I should have left it on, across my chest like I always do but I wanted to read my book, the latest Kate Atkinson, only just started it so can't even tell you what it's about. It's another Jackson Brodie so it'll be good for sure. Can't help picturing Jason Isaacs now with his lovely blue eyes.

Need to find my bag. Get my mobile then I can ring Melissa and she can ring for help. It's fully-charged with plenty of credit. She's my ICE. In Case of Emergency. I was going to ask her to move in with me. Think she'd say "yes". They say something like this tests a relationship. You know, when one person's injured and will need rehabilitation but I'm lucky in that respect too. Melissa's a nurse. Senior. Not long had a promotion. That's where we met. At the hospital. I'm a bit accident prone, you see, although this is the worst one yet. Usually just come off my bike… bicycle not motorbike. Not going fast enough to cause any real damage.

It'll get light soon. That'll help. They'll be able to see where everyone is, not rely on torches.

You'd think there would be mobiles ringing. Everyone uses mobiles, don't they? Shout too loudly because of the noise, even quiet electric trains are noisy. That doesn't make sense. Quiet and noisy.

Hello? I'm here! Anyone? Can someone see my bag? I need to ring Melissa. Hello?

## The Thing And The Nameless Page

"What was that?" Willem-Alexander, the ten-minute-crowned king of the Netherlands, scanned the large state room.

His right-hand man, a strange-looking tall thin Englishman called Enoch Barron-Smythe, followed his employer's gaze. "Sorry your… Highness? I can't see…"

"There! Over there!" The king pointed towards one of the gold and red embossed wallpapered walls.

"May I ask, sir, what I might be looking for?"

"There! There! That thing! What is it?"

"Oh yes. I see… I don't rightly know, sir. Perhaps it's a–"

"Spy!"

"Spy, sir? I highly doubt that."

"Someone catch it! Over there before it flies to the… you there! Shut the window!"

A page, whose name no one knew and who had almost nodded off during the ceremony which had taken place on the hottest day in the Netherlands' history, leapt to his feet and bolted for the window.

He'd not been able to see the 'thing' either but knew he had to do as he told or he'd follow the way of the last page who had missed fulfilling an order and had been turfed out with the recycling. Rumour had it that he'd had to put it out en-route but there had been no witnesses to confirm that, or none who would tell him.

After he shut the window, the page felt something buzz past his ear. He swung round to see the tiny flapping of wings and an electronic hum.

"Catch it!" he heard as he watched the 'thing' fly towards another open window so he bolted again and managed to get to the window before it reached it. Thwarted again it, hovered and spun in circles looking for other exits. Using his initiative, the boy did the same and shut all the other windows.

The room's gaze then loomed on the door, seconds before the thing spotted it.

"The door!" the king shouted and two sentries who had been chatting about which maid-in-waiting they'd get off with at the next door after-ceremony party, slammed the front door which such force that it made the twelve-tier cake, the centrepiece of the festivities, wobble.

Encouraged by his earlier success, the page ran after the 'thing', remembering a bag of treats he had in his pockets for the king's Smoushonds, he retrieved it, threw out the treats – oblivious to the resulting scurrying of claws along the newly polished floor – and lunged at the 'thing', wrapping it expertly in the bag, twisting the top so it had no chance of escape.

His heart thumped as the object battled to get out. Eventually, the thrashing subsided and the page realised the only sound he could hear was his heart thumping.

He looked up, around the room, and realised that everyone was staring at him. He swallowed, then as the king beckoned him, the page stepped forward, slowly, head lowered, inching step-by-step.

"Bring it here!" the king boomed and the page quickened along the long old room.

"Run, man!"

So the page did as he was told, the bag bumping in his hands, a squeak escaping from it as he did so.

When he reached the king, he stopped, held out his hands and bowed his head.

Not sure what to do now, knowing it would likely escape if he undid the bag, the king called on Barron-Smythe.

"I… er, don't know sir. Perhaps if–"

"Anyone else?" the king boomed, looking around the room. His gaze stopped on a short red-faced man standing near to where the king had first spotted the 'thing'.

"You!" the king shouted. "Step forward."

The flushed-faced man looked to his left, right, then pointed to his chest.

"Yes, you! Step forward."

The man did as he was told.

"You look familiar. What's your name?"

"Herbert, sir."

"Herbert… Herbert what?"

"Herbert Wintergrund, sir… your Highness."

"Sir is fine. Who are you?"

"I'm your science advisor, sir."

"Oh yes, so you are. You look shifty. What's the matter with you?"

"I… erm. That…" He looked over at the bag the page was still holding.

"Yes. Go on! What about it?"

"It's… I'm sorry, sir, but it's mine."

"Yours? What is it?"

"It's a new type of robot, sir. A present from the Herschel Space Observatory. For you. They thought you might like one – it does all sorts of clever things – and…"

"And?"

"I was going to put it with all your other presents next door but I was late arriving so I stuffed it into my pocket. The little blighter… sorry, your Highness. It escaped and well, went for the light."

The man's face was getting redder and redder, and the page wondered whether he might explode at any moment but then the king burst out laughing.

He clapped his hands twice, whistled for his dogs, and announced that there was enough food next door to feed an army and that they might even play pass the parcel before the disco started.

## A Scientifically Unexplained Occurrence

"Science? What do I know about science?"

"Make something up."

"I could do but… won't they know?"

"You're clever. You'll think of something."

"I don't think I'm that clever."

"You might surprise yourself."

"But twenty thousand words. If it was two thousand then maybe…"

"Just do it, Sawyer."

"Okay. But don't say I didn't warn you."

"Yeah, whatever."

The Bermuda Triangle. It's been written about to death. Pardon the pun. If all the experts in the world and Wikipedia subscribers can't come up with an explanation then how am I…? I could say some kind of boat-eating creature but then that would be as ridiculous as… the Loch Ness Monster. And even **I** know that doesn't exist.

Talking to my editor is never a pleasant experience. She's too much like my mother. Not mine necessarily but *a* mother. She's… mothering, smothering. But she pays the bills so she is 'she who must be obeyed' so that's what I do.

At least this time, she's given me a month to do it. And £5000. She never gives me that kind of budget. Unless she… oh no. She wants me to go there. Without ordering me. Sending me to my doom. That wouldn't tick her health and safety boxes.

I guess I could go to the area, interview the locals, get their spin on it. A couple of weeks on a tropical island wouldn't hurt. I could do a quick piece. Twenty k doesn't actually take long when you get going.

I've done NaNoWriMo three times. It's that 50,000 words in a month, you know… start first November, stop thirty-first with 50,000 words (or more in my case) in between. Thirty. Of course. See, I can't even remember that November hath thirty days, and all that.

So as I was saying, a couple of weeks on a tropical island… is Bermuda tropical? At least that's geography not science… sort of.

Okay, let's see. All-inclusive packages. A week? No. Who goes somewhere like that for a week? Three weeks, that's more like it. God, that's cheap. Oh yeah, I see why now. Tonight. Well, I suppose I could. Nothing stopping me here. No animals, plants half-dead anyway, and I could get Mrs Roberts… Robbins? Robinson? to come in and water them.

I've got a spare key under the mat. Yeah, I know, not very original. There's nothing much to steal anyway but that's not the point. I should move it. I will when I give it to Mrs R. Her garden's immaculate so she might get them blooming again. Or take them hostage. She can keep them, I don't mind. I'll probably get plastic ones, or silk – they're nicer; less… shiny.

Okay. So, nine pm it is. That gives me… be at the airport for seven… can't be doing with being late. Some people don't like all that hanging around and they'd rather queue than check in and do a bit of take-your-time shopping. Latest bestseller, cosy chair, a beer, a nice barmaid to chat to.

So, seven p.m. there, six p.m. leave. That gives me… yes, seven hours. Shower, pack… that's easy. Jeans to travel, shorts and loud t-shirts… look like a tourist.

Foreigners love spilling their deepest darkest secrets if they think there's some money in it. And with a budget like mine that'll buy a lot of wagging tongues. Four and a half grand left.

And Savannah won't be expecting many receipts. We do what we have to in this line of work. Beats accounting. That's what I used to do, by the way; finance manager for a small and not very successful stationery company. Got out before they went under.

Of course I was best placed to see that, wasn't I? I'd been writing on the side for a while so had built up a bit of a nest egg already. I know what you're thinking; finance, a position of trust, siphon something off the top but I'm not like that. Some are, granted, but not me.

Straight as a dye, whatever that means… metalwork? Oh, thanks Google. That's why I turned in that couple – at the tennis court. Well, it wasn't fair on the dog. Just because I don't have one myself it doesn't mean…

So now the only figures I want to be staring at all day are bikini-clad ones. Long, lean, tanned ones. Mismatching tops and bottoms with just a little of their bottoms… You get the picture.

It's good to be home… nothing missing. Not that Mrs… whatever-her-name-is is that type but I had expected the plants… hello boys, you **are** looking healthy. Glad I brought her something back now.

The article's done, emailed to the wicked witch, good old Wi-Fi. It seems obvious now you think about it; City of Atlantis underneath the Bermuda Triangle. All those people heading down to the city that doesn't sleep. Now that was a holiday I won't forget in a hurry.

## It Wasn't Me

*This went on to become part of my dog detective novel 'Oh, Henry'*

Gwynne looked down at the ripped toy, then into the big brown eyes staring up at her.

"It wasn't me."

"Really? Then who was it? There's only you and I here."

The big brown eyes kept staring. "Alright. I confess. It was me but it's your fault for–"

"Henry! You've become so cheeky since we gave you the ability to talk."

Henry wagged his tail.

Gwynne was pretty sure that had enhanced since they, her and her boss, Dr Temple Moss, had injected the dog with the experimental speech drugs. "I thought that toy was your favourite."

"I was only playing."

"It's got dribble all over it. You were shaking it weren't you?"

Henry nodded. "It's what we do. We're dogs. We chase rabbits, cats and things."

"Anything that moves, I know."

"So you give me a cat toy and I'm going to–"

"Chase, Henry. You didn't need to rip it to shreds."

"It's not shreds. An ear's come off, that's all."

"What did I say about you being cheeky?"

"Just speaking my mind."

"If I'd known…"

"What?"

"Nothing. Never mind. Now, Dr Moss and I have some things we want you to do. When we ask you questions, we want your honest answers, okay?"

Henry nodded.

Right on cue, Dr Moss entered the lab, studying a clipboard. "How is he today?"

"I'm well, thank you."

Dr Moss looked up from his notes. "Henry?"

Henry smiled. "That's me."

"So everything's okay. Voice alright?"

"More than alright," Gwynne answered. "Can't shut him up."

"I did think it was weird to start with," Henry said. "I could hear myself. Of course I could always hear myself but it's like it was clearer, louder and…"

Dr Moss watched Henry's lips move as he waffled on. "Your lips are moving."

Henry stopped mid-stream. "Of course. I'm no ventriloquist."

Dr Moss laughed, looked at Gwynne's scowl and laughed again.

Henry turned to Gwynne. "You said you had some questions?"

"Yes. Dr Moss?"

The doctor looked back down at his clipboard. "Number one. How do you feel?"

Henry frowned and repeated, "I'm well, thank you."

"Number two. Has anything else improved since the implementation of the medication?"

"'implementation of the medication'," Henry mimicked. "Like what?"

"Memory? Vocabulary? Desires? Motivations?"

"Erm…"

"Maybe a bit too much all at once," Gwynne suggested.

"No, it's okay," Henry said. "Memory. The same, I think. Born, eat, poop, chew…" He looked at the toy. "I couldn't help it."

"That's okay, Henry," Dr Moss soothed. "That's what they're there for. Any frustrations?"

"Apart from it not being a real cat?"

Dr Moss laughed and put a large tick in the 'sense of humour' box.

"You asked about vocabulary," Henry continued.

"Yes," Gwynne butted in. "And Desires, Motivation."

"Vocabulary. Now I like hearing the sound of my voice–"

"We can tell," Gwynne mumbled, receiving a dirty look from Henry.

"It's not like I've studied a dictionary since you gave me that stuff."

"Interesting," Dr Moss said while chewing on the end of his pen.

Henry didn't find that interesting at all. He'd quite like to spend his time studying not only a dictionary but an encyclopaedia as well, but thought that a step too far at this early stage. "As for desires. I still desire to rip up…" He looked up at Gwynne and paused. "Desire to play with my toys. That was an accident. Motivation, being given a fake cat is a good one."

"Very good." The doctor nodded and jotted more notes. "Question four. If you could be any animal what would you be?"

Henry tilted his head.

"Would you like me to repeat that?"

Henry straightened his head again. "You mean you can change me into something else?"

Dr Moss laughed. "Of course not, Henry. We can only work with what we have."

"That's a silly question then isn't it?"

"It's hypothetical."

Henry wished he'd had that dictionary.

"Pretend," Gwynne added, seeing the expression on his face.

"A giraffe."

The two white-jacketed humans looked at each other then back at Henry.

"A giraffe?" Gwynne asked.

"Why a giraffe, Henry?"

"It's obvious, isn't it?"

The doctor shook his head.

"Because all I see all day are ankles. Knees if I'm begging, which I don't plan on doing again any time soon, by the way. If I was… were a giraffe I'd be able to see anything, wouldn't I? Even more than you. Any more questions?"

Dr Moss nodded. "A few but I think that's enough for today."

Gwynne looked at him startled, so he beckoned for her to join him in the corridor.

Henry watched them leave then turned his attention to the one-eared cat. "They'll be giving that stuff to you next, although they'd have to sew your ear back on or you wouldn't be able to hear their questions properly."

He then looked back at the glass pane in the door, saw the ecstatic expression on Gwynne and the doctor's faces. "If you're like that now, just wait until I show you what I can **really** do."

## In His Shoes

Looking out through the office window, Eden pictured herself in Miguel's shoes then told herself off when she saw the image of her size fives comically floating around in his elevens.

She didn't know he was elevens, of course, being a colleague, but he was tall, and tall men usually had big feet. She smuggled a laugh remembering what big feet implied, but harking back to previous boyfriends, she figured it was a lie made up by a man who should have had very small feet.

Not the time to joke, she told herself as she watched Miguel wobble. Now was the time to have small feet, hers balancing on the ledge instead of his. She wanted to get nearer, to speak to him, but the MD, Steve, had told them to keep back.

She wondered who had made Miguel go out there. It was always a 'who', rarely a 'what'. A spurned love, crippling debt caused by a spurned love. She didn't know Miguel that well so couldn't recall any mention of a love, spurned or otherwise.

Someone next to her was crying. Turning round, Eden spotted Hayley, the accounts assistant, sobbing into a wad of tissues, mascara running down her face.

She couldn't imagine her and Miguel being an item and knew how easily Hayley burst into tears; a missing cat, broken arm, missed appointment, none of them hers.

Steve was consoling her, or trying to, her wailing getting louder, and looking at Miguel, Eden saw this was making him more nervous.

With Steve distracted, Eden knew this was her chance, so she casually walked towards the open window and leaned out, just a little. "Hi, Miguel."

Miguel screamed and clung on to the metal window edging. Behind her, Hayley screamed.

"Sorry," Eden whispered.

Miguel said nothing.

"Hi, Miguel," Eden repeated, this time quieter.

"Hello, Eden."

"Can I ask a silly question?"

"Please go back inside."

"I prefer it out here."

"So do I."

"This silly question..."

"I know what you're going to ask. What am I doing out here?"

"No, that wasn't it. I can see what you're doing."

"Okay, 'why then'."

"And your answer is..."

"Because I've had enough."

"Of..."

"Eden, please go back inside. This was supposed to be quick and before anyone got to work but..."

"You can't do it."

"I will. I'll jump."

"But you haven't yet."

"You're not helping."

"Okay. I'll go back in–"

"No! Stay!"

"The police will be shortly."

"Oh, God."

"Wouldn't it be better to come inside before they do? Say it's all been a big mistake."

"No."

"Why 'no'?"

"They'd arrest me."

"The two other options open to you would be worse."

"Two?"

"Still being out here when they do arrive, or being a splat when they do."

"Don't say that."

"What? Splat?"

Miguel nodded.

"You're on a fifth-storey ledge with nothing but concrete to break your fall. How did you think you'd end up?"

"I didn't think..."

"Seriously?"

"It just seemed like..."

"The right thing to do?"

Miguel nodded again.

"Why?"

Miguel shrugged then screamed as his right foot slipped sideways, his shoe falling to the ground with a sickening thud.

"See, that could have been you," Eden said, then wondered whether it was the right thing to say. Seeing Miguel was struggling to balance in his socked right foot said, "Take your sock off, there's no grip."

"I can't."

"You'll fall if you don't."

"I can't bend down."

"I'll go and get your shoe then."

"No! Don't leave me."

"I'll send someone else."

Miguel shook his head, gently, both hands gripping to the window edges. "I'll just stay still."

"You can't do that forever."

"I know."

"Then we'll have to come up with a plan B. What size shoes do you take?"

"Eight."

"Okay. Back in a tick."

"Don't!..."

But Eden had disappeared.

"Steve. What size shoes do you take?"

"Ten. Why?"

"That'll have to do. I need your right one."

"What? Why?"

"Please."

"Okay," Steve said and handed Eden his right shoe.

"Miguel. Put this on, it's going to be a bit big but wiggle your foot to the front for grip."

"I can't move."

"It's fine. Your right foot's on the ledge. Just hold on tighter and lift your foot up a little. I'll lean out, position it and you put your foot in it."

"This is crazy."

"Yes, it is, but not as crazy as you coming out here in the first place."

"I never knew you were such a bossy boots."

"When the situation demands it. Now lift."

As Miguel lifted his foot, Eden hovered the shoe underneath it and Miguel wedged his foot to the front of the shoe. Eden seized the opportunity to grab him and pull him into the office where their colleagues crowded round them, all talking, one crying, at once. Steve then took charge and led Miguel and Eden to his office.

After prolonged questioning by Steve and the police, a check-up at hospital and counselling sessions booked, Miguel was released into Eden's care and it wasn't long before she found out that the size debate really wasn't true.

## Do It Right Or Get Off The Horse

"Do it right or get off the horse."

India burst into tears.

"Oh, Indy. Don't be such a cry baby."

"Edward!" Sophie glared at her husband, picked their daughter off the rocking horse and carried her into one of the adjoining upstairs rooms of the old rambling house.

Edward followed without replying.

"You're turning into your p…" Sophie hesitated. "No, I'm not going to say it. They're trying."

"Yes, dear, sometimes they are… very."

Sophie smiled, ice cracking.

"I'm just trying to instil into her that if you're going to do something then you should do it 100% – no half measures."

"But she's only eighteen months old."

"They say to start young."

"I think that's languages, Edward."

His eyes lit up.

"No, Edward."

"Decus et tutamen," Edward said, walking towards India who was sitting on an overgrown royal-blue sofa, playing with a toy giraffe. Looking up, she burst into tears again.

Edward looked over at his wife.

"It's not my fault," she said. "I guess you look too much like your brother."

"Which one?... Oh, he scares her that much?"

"I think it's his ears."

Edward thought for a moment then put one of his fingers in the air. "Ah, ha!"

Sophie watched him leave the room. She waited. And waited.

Finally, he returned with a mobile in one hand and catalogue in the other.

"Yes, hello. I'd like to order item number… 117342E please. Size? Oh. Erm, the largest you have. Yes, certainly. Oh. Account number…"

Sophie watched him flick back to the inside front page.

"HRH001." He laughed. "And how quickly do you… really? Yes, fifteen minutes would be fantastic. You have the home address. Okay, well, thank you. Goodbye."

Turning to India, he said, "Indy. Daddy's got a present for you."

The little girl's eyes widened followed by a toothy grin. Discarding the giraffe, she held out both hands, palms up.

Sophie laughed. "Daddy's girl after all."

Edward walked over to a large Queen Anne table, picked up a remote and zapped it at an impressive TV situated in one corner of the room.

At the sound of 'In the Night Garden' theme tune, India squealed and turned her head round in an owl-like fashion. Sophie walked over to her and turned her body to face the TV.

India looked up at her mother and chuckled, then the family sat together as the programme started.

A knock at the door soon distracted them and the girls watched as Edward walked towards a man in a smart black uniform as he brought in a huge brown cardboard box. Edward pointed at the floor by the sofa.

India screamed and jumped down, lunging herself at the box.

"Would you like me to open it for you, sir?" the man asked.

"Oh no," Edward said a little too dramatically, turning to India. "That would spoil all the fun wouldn't it?"

India nodded seriously.

The uniformed man bowed his head at Edward, who thanked him, and the man left the room.

Edward picked up India while Sophie pulled at the ends of the Hamley's picture parcel tape to loosen them, then sat on the sofa as India, with Edward hovering over the box, did the rest.

As the strips came off, a gigantic grey and pink nose shot out of the top.

India screamed and buried her head into Edward's chest.

"It's okay," he soothed, and, with one hand, tucked over the two cardboard lids until they sat limply by the side of the box. He then turned India to face the top so she could see what the nose was attached to. She immediately giggled.

Sophie stood up and the three of them peered into the dark space.

"Oh, Edward," Sophie laughed, "that's hilarious."

Edward then handed India to Sophie while he leaned over the box to take the creature out of its cardboard enclosure. India's eyes watched his every move.

As its tail finally appeared, she squealed and held out her hands as Edward placed it on the floor and moved the box out the way.

Sophie sat her gently next to the beast and joined Edward on the sofa.

India started with a hug, then flicked its tail, pretended to walk its feet along the priceless Egyptian rug, then clasped its trunk making a distinctly cow-like moo.

"Mr Elephant doesn't moo, Indy," Edward said.

"Ellie," India replied.

"Yes, Indy, he's an elephant."

India shook her head.

Edward and Sophie nodded theirs.

"Ellie," India repeated. "Ellie… girl."

"Oh," Sophie said. "She's a girl."

"Like you, Indy," Edward added.

India nodded, then sighed, turned to look at the cardboard box, and stood up.

"It's empty," Edward said as India started walking towards it.

"All gone," Sophie confirmed.

India craned her neck to try to see inside the box but wasn't tall enough.

Sophie stood, walked over to her and tipped the box on to one side so that the open top faced them. "See," she said.

But India wasn't listening. She walked into the box, sat down and thrust out her arms.

"Brmmm!" she shouted. "Brmmm, brmmm."

Sophie laughed and turned to Edward, who was frowning. "Buy her the most expensive toy on the planet," she said, "and she turns a cardboard box into a car. Now that's clever."

## Carry on With the Show

The music played despite Leslie not being there. He was supposed to be giving a speech, recounting his brother's life – the good times. It wouldn't have taken him long.

Father Orburn hoped he'd show before Beethoven stopped, or at least during his introduction, the formulaic words ingrained into his memory, just names to be slotted in.

As the last few bars of Moonlight Sonata rang out, the doors to the crematorium hall burst open and a drunken Leslie staggered in, still clutching a half-empty bottle of Jack Daniels.

"She'll be coming round the mountains" weren't the words Father Orburn had been hoping to come out of Leslie Bristow's mouth but they certainly lifted the mood… that, and Leslie's pink pyjamas.

Father Orburn wondered if the brothers had made a pact to see each other off in style… a dare, or a simple case of Leslie not taking Ardal's death very well, or perhaps too well.

Leslie slumped down onto a half-empty pew, winked at the vicar and put up one thumb, to which Father Orburn began his introduction.

As he spoke, he wondered whether he'd be best to miss out Leslie, move on to Ardal's son or the neighbour, but Leslie was looking so earnestly at every word that the vicar decided it was worth the risk, despite Leslie's wiggling bottom.

Had there not been a schedule to keep to, Father Orburn would have suggested a nature break, so it was service as normal, or abnormal in this case.

"And now a few words from Leslie." The two men looked at each other. "Leslie?"

Leslie turned round, looked back at the crematorium doors, then faced front, to the vicar. "Oh, right!" he said in his loud Irish accent and went to stand up but swayed like a toy Hawaiian dancer stuck to a car's dashboard, and sat down again.

"Perhaps Ardal's son…" the vicar started but stopped as Leslie made a second attempt to stand. A lady further along the pew rushed to his aid and walked him slowly up the aisle to the front of the hall.

Once in situ, the lady returned to her seat, leaving Leslie leaning heavily against the lectern, almost tipping it over. Father

Orburn lunged forward to save it but Leslie pulled it back and stood upright, as if on parade.

Taking a deep breath, Leslie went to speak but closed his mouth again. A child in the congregation began laughing but was swiftly quietened.

Leslie looked at the vicar as if for a cue.

"You were going to say a few words about Ardal?"

Leslie nodded. "Ardal…" He paused and looked down at the lectern.

The vicar was about to speak again when Leslie resumed.

"Ardal!" he boomed, "No one knew Ardal like I knew Ardal."

The vicar and Dermot, Ardal's son, exchanged glances, both men stepping forward, ready to take over if necessary, Father Orburn hoping that Leslie wouldn't burst into song.

"Ardal!" Leslie said even louder, but stopped as Dermot tapped his arm. "I'm sorry, son," Leslie bellowed, "I should have told you all those years ago. You had a right to know."

"I think we should go outside," Dermot said, pulling Leslie's arm.

"No! I want everyone to hear this. That you're Ardal's son."

"I know, Uncle Leslie."

"I know you know."

Dermot screwed up his face and tugged at Leslie's arm again.

"It's okay," Leslie continued. "Everything's going to be fine. You come home with me and…"

"Uncle Leslie. I have my own house. Have had for…"

"Oh, that's right."

Father Orburn coughed dramatically and Leslie put up his right index finger. "Sorry, your honour. Won't be a minute. Now, Dermot. The time has come for the truth, for everyone to know that your father… that your father…"

"Yes?" Dermot said.

"That Ardal… I… the coffin."

Everyone looked at the coffin.

"That the man in the coffin isn't Ardal."

"What?" Dermot growled at Leslie.

"I mean…" Leslie continued nervously, "It's Leslie in there, not Ardal."

"Dermot," Father Orburn interrupted. "I think you'd better see your uncle…"

"I'm not his uncle!" Leslie shouted. "I'm his father! I'm Ardal!"

The child who'd earlier been laughing promptly burst into tears accompanied by gasps around the congregation.

"He…" the newly confessed Ardal pointed to the coffin, "Leslie was called up, you see, and well, he didn't want to go. I wasn't, don't know why, but I wanted to go so we swapped places. He said he'd look after Virginia and… you were only a nipper. Turns out he looked after her too well and they… she knew but never said anything and by the time I came back, you were a family. Everyone believed them… wouldn't believe me when I tried to tell the truth, they said the war had damaged my brain and… I loved you… loved you both, even Leslie despite what he did, so I went along with it. I still got to see you but it wasn't the same…"

"So why now? Why the pink pyjamas?" Dermot asked.

"It was your mother's and my song. It was playing when we met, Leslie knew and…"

"I'm sorry," Father Orburn said. "But we should…"

Dermot smiled. "My father or not, Dad would have loved to have seen you in those so, sure, Father Orburn. Carry on with the show."

## Me, Myself And I

It'll be lunchtime soon. When they come round rattling the trolleys, waking up the old dears. Most of them can only just remember having breakfast. 'Cause all they do is sleep. TV's on full blast. Wouldn't wake the dead in here.

My little Beau came to see me yesterday. Got a promotion, he said. Assistant manager. Pleased as punch, I was. Told him how proud. He blushed like a schoolboy. I remember when he wore short trousers. He had the funniest of knees. All knotted like an old oak tree. Hated swimming 'cause of his knees. Probably why he's gone a bit porky.

Still, he's got a girlfriend so he doesn't have to worry. She probably feeds him too much anyway. Not met her yet. He says she's shy but how shy can she be? I'm only his old mum. Wouldn't hurt a nit, I wouldn't.

Suppose she's busy. Social worker or something like that, he said. She'll be run off her feet. Just look at the specimens that come visiting in here. No control on their kids. Let them run around making all that noise.

'Course no one takes a blind bit of notice. But then they wouldn't, would they? Half of them don't hear and the other half can't see past the warts on their noses. Oh my god, some of them are so ugly. Urgh. Worse than that Queen Grimhilde in Snow White.

We've got a resident called Hilda and she is grim. Face on her like… well, worse than the back end of a bus, but then so would you if you'd got through six husbands. Six! Who'd marry her once, let alone six times?

Of course, I only had the one husband. My Billy. Ooh he was lovely. The apple of my eye was Billy. Died in service. I couldn't be with anyone else after that. No one could match up to him, could they?

Not that he would have minded. Generous to a fault, was my William. He'd said that I should move on if anything happened to him. He wasn't to know that he'd be dead six months later, was he? I always thought it would be his work that would kill him.

But it was a career to him. Loved it, he did. "Can't see myself being anywhere else," he'd say, and he died doing what he loved.

The number twenty-seven it was. His bus. How ironic. Stepped out in front of it when his colleague was reversing. Didn't look, did he. Silly Billy. Still, he left me a good pension and I can't complain.

That Mrs Beech is at it again. I do wish she'd stop doing that. Drives me round the bend. Wish someone would take that remote control off her. Not that anyone's watching the damn thing anyway. I think they just like noise. The ones that can hear of course. And the ones that are awake.

The menu says it's going to be fish and chips. As long as the peas are garden and not the mushy slop we usually get. And the fish had better be breaded not battered. They do the batter too greasy. Don't like grease. Have to wash my hands afterwards. Makes my skin all blotchy and got to keep my skin clear, haven't I.

Never know when a Billy mark two might land here. They're all like aliens. Most of them on another planet, away with the fairies. Some believe in them too, others talk to them. I don't talk to no one. No one got nothing to say in here.

So I keep to myself. Me, myself and I. And that suits me just fine. The only time I get a decent conversation. Apart from my Beau but he's busy with his shop. He gets here when he can and I understand that.

Oh, and there's the lady with the library trolley. Margot. Bit barking, but lovely. Calls me Glenys. Keep telling her my name's Ginger but no, keeps calling me Glenys. Still, if it makes her happy. I just smile and she goes on her way to the next poor old soul.

Then there's Mr North, the manager. Always on my case about my room. "Can't have it looking like a tip, Mrs Rogers," he tells me.

"It's not a tip," I tell him. "It's my stuff. Got to have my stuff around me."

"But you've got to be respectful to Mrs Beech," he tells me.

"I am!" I say, but he won't listen. Nobody listens to me so I don't bother.

You soon learn in a place like this. Got experience, you see. Seen the insides of a few of these 'establishments'. Think they're doing us a favour by having us here but we pay for the privilege. My Billy's pension won't last forever, then I'll be out on my ear.

Never mind, Beau will see me right. I can look after him. Give him proper meals. None of that stodge or those little white boxes that you put in the microwave and zap to death so it hisses when it comes out the other end. Three square meals a day. That's what I was always taught. And it didn't do my Billy any harm.

Oh look, there's our lunch. Been nice speaking to you. Same time tomorrow? Lancashire hotpot then spotted dick for afters. Lovely.

## A Lot To Learn

There was something about being a city vet that always appealed to Marley, something about the delight on the children's faces when they saw a live animal, bigger than the stick insects, gerbils or cats they lived with.

Nothing, however, had prepared him for Brady 'What's that?' Smith.

"No one will take you seriously if you wear an Eeyore tie," Gina, Marley's girlfriend, had said that morning.

"I don't want them to take me seriously, they're children."

"What about their teachers? Aren't you supposed to be setting a good example?"

"AA Milne, Gina. There's nothing more wholesome than Winnie the Pooh."

"Eeyore."

"Exactly."

With that, she'd kissed him goodbye and gone off to her first day with Clampett, Lennox and Browne.

Marley rinsed his cereal bowl, grabbed his black bag, dropped the flat's Yale latch, then locked above and below it, something they'd never had to do at Broughton Heath.

As newlyweds they had little to steal but if the place didn't look secure it was an open invitation – or so said Nico and Rachel who'd moved to London a couple of years before, and whose neighbours had both been burgled.

So after checks bordering on OCD, Marley took the number twenty-seven bus, making a mental note of the route so he could walk it home.

Entering the surgery immediately felt comfortable, and Marley knew he'd made the right decision.

"Morning, Marley," his new boss, Quinn Sanderson, said before sipping a cup of steaming black coffee. "Want one?"

"Please."

"If you're quick, Imogen will get it for you… kitchen on the left, from then on you make your own. We all do."

"Sure. Thanks, Quinn."

"Good to have you on board. We've got Roehill Juniors today."

"Looking forward to it."

"Tell me that again later and I'll buy you a pint."

"Deal," Marley said, and disappeared into the kitchen.

Mug in hand, Marley was given a guided tour of the complex then shown to his office and given his itinerary for the day, with ten a.m. 'til noon blocked out for the school visit.

This left four early slots for patients: Muffin, a sock-swallowing Beagle; Roger, a sneezing rabbit (who it turns out was allergic to carrots); Daisy the Jack Russell for her first inoculations; and Kevin the fat hamster who turned out to be female, and fat for a very specific reason.

Marley was writing up Kevin's notes when he heard loud voices coming from the car park. Pulling up his blind, he saw a congregation of royal-blue-uniformed children running in circles, waving their hands and a couple playing patty cake.

There were two teachers with them, a tall blonde lady and a shorter black woman who stopped suddenly, making a couple of the children bump into her, then blew a whistle, the children immediately standing to attention.

With a click of her fingers, the children formed an orderly line and followed her and her colleague round the corner, towards the building's front door. Knowing he had a minute or two at the most, he finished his notes, screen-locked the computer, and headed out into reception to meet them.

The children were standing gazing up their teachers, the blonde woman talking to one of the receptionists, Pearl, who was pointing in Marley's direction.

"Thanks, Pearl," Marley said, and with a swoop of his arms, said, "Do follow me, ladies and gentlemen," and the teachers escorted the children, one adult at either end.

Marley walked past his office and the consulting rooms, and through a back door. Some of the children gasped and looked around at the array of animals; the pigs, cows and chickens being the nearest enclosures.

Marley turned to the two teachers. "Good morning, I'm Marley Sullivan. I'll be your guide for today. Any questions at all just let me know."

"By raising your hand," the blonde teacher said to the group, then turned to Marley. "Erin Rose, Mrs, and this is Mrs Jackson."

"Pleased to meet you, Mrs Rose, Mrs Jackson."

Mrs Jackson smiled briefly then clicked her fingers at a young boy who had started to wander off. "Keep in the group, Brady."

The boy duly returned but looked around him rather than at her.

Unsure as to what the children wanted to know, Marley showed them the first pen, a variety of chickens, and explained the different species, ensuring he didn't get too technical.

The pigs followed next and while some of the children stayed with Marley, the rest went on to the cows with their two teachers.

Brady stood closest to the pigs, in front of Marley, and started emulating their noises.

"Very good… Brady, is it?"

The boy nodded.

"You like pigs?" Marley asked.

The boy shrugged.

"You don't know?"

Brady shook his head.

"I like pigs," Marley said.

The boy said nothing but looked up at Marley.

"Do you eat bacon?"

The boy nodded eagerly.

"Ham sandwiches?"

He nodded again.

"Then you like pigs," Marley said, trying to be helpful.

The boy frowned.

"Bacon… ham… come from pigs and…" Marley stopped talking when the boy screwed up his face and started bawling. Marley went to crouch down to him, to console him, but Brady ran towards Mrs Rose and buried his face in her skirt.

Mrs Jackson stormed over to Marley. "What have you done?"

"I'm sorry, Mrs Jackson but he didn't seem to know what a pig was."

"And you told him?"

"I am a vet."

"And he's just a boy."

As Marley looked at Brady, he realised he had a lot to learn about children before he and Gina had any of their own.

## Oh Brother!

Ooh, I could swing for my brother sometimes. Dad says he's a blessing, an 'accident', but I think he's a curse. I'm supposed to look after him when Dad and Sarah, that's my step-mum, want to go out, but sod that!

I'm seventeen and should be having fun. Why should I stay in while my mates all go out? I'm left clearing up puke when brat eats too much ice cream or chocolate 'Buttons'. It's not my fault if he eats the whole packet in one go!

I try to study while brat pretends he's a train or an aeroplane or something equally loud and infuriating. Sarah hears me shouting at him to "eff off" and swishes into the room, her blonde hair swaying and annoyingly shiny. She whisks him away, singing his favourite; 'The Mockingbird Song', giving me a glare that could freeze a volcano. I'm in her bad books, but so what? It does the trick…gets brat out of my way.

I switch off the PC and look up as Sarah returns, now smiling sweetly. She reminds me that she and Dad are going out tonight and that I'm "not asked to baby-sit very often"…not very often, my arse! "Yes, Mum"…she likes me to call her 'Mum' and thinks it means something to me.

Of course it doesn't. My real mum, Celia, died when I was seven. If Sarah thinks that playing a mother to me for four years makes her my mum then she can go to – "I haven't forgotten!" I add as an afterthought and mimic her sickly smile.

Her glare returns. She leaves the room, muttering something under her breath. I catch the words "always" and "mood", and a 'tut' or two.

The front door slams signifying Dad's arrival. "Hello Button," I hear. Brat's obviously in sight. I skip downstairs in a 'Little House on the Prairie' fashion (Sarah watches it on UK Gold, the lazy cow).

He's looking very smart in his charcoal grey city-style pinstripe suit. I'm greeted with a "Hello Poppet" as he plants a kiss on my right cheek. He asks me how my studies are going and beams as I say they're all done.

Sarah looks at me in a "as little as you can get away with" expression but I don't care. She can't tell me what to do.

Sarah reminds Dad that they're running late and he rushes upstairs to get changed. Poor Dad, the stick she gives him. Nag, nag, nag. I wouldn't be like her; not that I'm ever going to get married and I'll certainly never have kids!

With the car scrunching its way out of the drive and brat despatched to bed, I settle on the sofa with some smuggled-in cider, Galaxy Fruit & Nut and 'Final Destination four' on DVD.

I get to a quiet bit of the film, about half way through, press the pause button on the remote and go to check on the kid, as I'd promised Dad. Brat's sleeping soundly. *Makes a change*, I think.

Glancing in the bathroom mirror on the way back downstairs, I make a mental note to get pink streaks in my hair like Penny at school – Sarah would hate that. Dad's a pushover. He lets me do whatever I want – says I'm a teenager and I'm going through a 'phase'. Phases are a great excuse to get away with murder!

I leap down the stairs, missing the last couple of steps and settle back on the sofa, finishing off the cider. The film's nearly finished when the doorbell rings. I swear, stuff the empty cider bottle under a cushion, and press the pause button.

With the chain on as instructed, I open the front door and see my dad's brother, Mike, standing in front of me. "Hiya!" I beam but he looks awful. I see tears streaming down his face and know something's really wrong.

"What's happened?" I ask, dreading his words. I feel sick and shiver. He just says, "I'm sorry, Janie, so sorry. Can I come in?" I say nothing but take the chain off and move back so he can get past.

He asks me to sit down but I can't. I stand fixed as if super-glued to the spot. Mike tries to blink his tears away without much success. He puts his arms around me, easing me on to the sofa.

He clears his throat and begins to explain that my dad was driving to the restaurant when a lorry pulled out of a side road and the car hit it head on. "I'm so sorry, Janie," Mike says again. "They didn't stand a chance."

After a pause, he asks me if he can get me a drink. I shake my head. I say I want to see my dad but Uncle Mike drops his head. He clasps my hands and continues. "Aunt Nola's getting the spare room ready for you to stay with us. You wait here, I'll switch everything off, fetch you some clothes and get your brother."

In a haze, I trudge upstairs while Mike switches the TV off, followed by lights in the lounge and kitchen. I head for the box room. Leaning over the small bed and stroking a slip of Tyler's hair from his forehead, I whisper "Sorry, little one, but you're stuck with me now. Don't worry. I'll look after you."

Tears roll down my face as I sing, "Hush, little baby. Don't say a word. Mama's going to buy you a mocking bird." and I suddenly realise that I'm not only crying for Dad but also for Sarah – my second mum.

## Leaving A Gap

~~Hello diary.~~ Hello Diary. Mum bought you for me for Christmas and I'm so excited. I ~~doh~~ ~~doent~~ don't know whether to wait until January the first or start now. Next year is a whole week away and we've had such a great Christmas Day so I think I'm going to start now. I am. Okay, new line.

Dad was being a bit quiet today. I think he ate too much. So did I.

Mum was busy cooking so hers was colder than ours because she wanted to do the washing up before she had hers and she had less than us, I don't think she was hungry. She told us not to wait so we didn't. I felt a bit bad but Dad said we should do as we were told so we did. I didn't eat as quickly as him because I wanted to still be eating when Mum came to the table.

Oh yes, you won't know that the kitchen table is now in the dining room. Yes, we have a dining room! So the kitchen table is now the dining room table. I don't think it minds. In fact I think it's really happy.

I'm happy too because I like it here. It's bigger than our old flat. This one has an upstairs, where we sleep, which means I have to come downstairs if I need a drink of water when I can't sleep.

Mum suggested – suggested means that she was giving me a good idea – but I didn't think it was a good idea so I did not do it. She suggested that I take a glass of water to bed, when I go to bed, but it'll get warm. I said that to her and she said it was okay.

This place is warmer than the flat. It has fancy white windows with two pieces of glass in each one! So I didn't bring any water to bed. I don't mind getting up and going to the kitchen because I get cold and my bed is still warm when I get back.

I'm going to say goodnight now because I'm tired and it's late. Nearly ten o'clock. If I get up to get some water, I might say hello but nothing will have happened for me to report other than me going downstairs and getting the water so I probably won't.

~~Good morning diary. It is December the 26th.~~

December 26 – Boxing Day

Good morning Diary. I forgot that diaries have the dates at the top so I've gone back to yesterdays and put December 25 – Christmas Day at the top, just in little writing because I didn't leave much space.

This is not a normal diary because it doesn't have the dates at the top. Mum said she didn't want to buy me one of those because it would mean that I could only write on one page and she said I should write whatever I wanted.

She called it a journal – she helped me spell it – but it sounds silly to say Hello Journal so I have called ~~it~~ you a Diary. Not a diary with a little d because you are a person like me because when I read you, you talk to me.

There are lines so I can write straight. I like it. I try to make my handwriting nice, like I was ~~teached~~ tort at school. That was a long time ago. I'm too old to go to school now.

Nothing really happens at home so I don't know if I would fill a whole page anyway but it does mean that I can put two days on one page if I want to. I left a gap on yesterdays because we had a busy day so I can tell you what happened. I will do it later. I will not forget. I have a good memory.

Mum is calling me to go downstairs for breakfast so I am going now but I will write more later.

----

I have put a line there because it means that I am not here for a while.

December 28 – The Day After The Day After Boxing Day

Sorry I have not written anything for two days. I have left lots of lines so I can write what happened yesterday. I have put in the title. December 27 – The Day After Boxing Day but I don't want to write it yet.

I think you will want to know what happened so I will put a little ~~now~~ here.

Mum has left us. I think that's why Dad was quiet but he has not said much. He said she packed a few things in a bag and left in the middle of the night. I wanted to go into their bedroom to see which things she took. She showed me her clothes so I know which ones are missing but Dad will not let me. I asked him when she left, what time, but he ~~shaked~~ shook his head.

I said before, to you, that I usually wake up and get a glass of water but I didn't. I would have seen her leave, tried to stop her. I would have woken up if she left ~~would not I~~?

I think it's going to be okay. Just with Dad and I. Mum did the cooking ~~and shopping~~ and cleaning but I can do that. I can do the cooking. I watched Mum. I can clean too. I know what to do.

Dad will do the shopping. Sometimes he goes to the pub for a drink. ~~He is not a alko~~ He does not drink much. He asked me if I wanted to go with him but I don't like to go out.

I have to go. Dad wants me. He needs me. So I am leaving a gap.

## A Broken Dart / Of Moonlight – Splintered On The Sea

Cassie took a deep breath. “A broken dart of moonlight – splintered on the sea…”

Landon laughed, spluttering into his tea.

“What’s wrong with that?” Cassie replied, her voice barely a whisper.

“Prose of the deepest hue.”

“Sorry?”

“Purple prose. It’s a phrase we use in class when something’s over dramatic, too… how do I put this delicately? Flowery.”

Marina piped up from the back of the staff room. “You couldn’t be delicate if you tried, Landon.”

Blythe, who’d been making her and Cassie’s teas, resisted the urge to defend Cassie, glad that Marina had come to the rescue, as she so often did.

“Give her a break,” Marina continued. “She’s not trying to write Shakespeare.”

“Just as well,” Landon replied, “I didn’t like his stuff the first time round.”

“And you call yourself an English teacher?”

“No,” Landon laughed, “that’s what Teresa Harkett calls me.”

Right on cue, the headmistress walked into the room.

Cassie and Marina stood up. Blythe looked in their direction, still wondering why Teresa provoked that reaction. They weren’t students. Respect, yes, but it bordered on… she wasn’t sure.

Fright? No, too… dramatic. But it wasn’t reverence. In the three months Blythe had been there, no one had explained to her why Teresa was such a force to be reckoned with.

She’d been nothing but sweet to Blythe. Two sides of a coin, she guessed; sweet to the new ones, something quite different to those accustomed. Blythe absentmindedly dropped the teaspoon onto the draining board which turned the room’s attention to her.

“Morning everyone… Blythe,” Teresa said. “Cassie, Landon, can I have a word please.”

The two teachers looked at each other, Cassie blushed.

Teresa looked at the sink. “You can bring your teas with you.”

Silently, Blythe handed one of the mugs to Cassie, who smiled then followed Landon and Teresa to the Head's Office.

"Sit down please," Teresa said, more of an order than request.

They did as they were told, waiting for her to speak, or at least sit. She did neither.

Landon opened his mouth but shut it again.

"Right," Teresa said finally. "You're probably wondering why I've asked you here."

Cassie and Landon looked at each other as if 'ask' had anything to do with it. Landon recognised the phrasing from somewhere but couldn't place it. Landon winked at Cassie who giggled.

"It's come to my attention," Teresa continued.

Uh oh, Cassie thought, this never ends well.

"It's come to my attention," Teresa repeated, returning Landon's gaze which she could see was veering towards the window.

"Yes, Teresa, listening," Landon grinned.

Cassie could only admire his cheek, knowing she'd never be so brave… or stupid.

"As I said," Teresa tried again. "It has come to my attention…"

Cassie gulped; three times wasn't good.

"…that the English literature students aren't performing as well as they could be."

Cassie stifled a smile at the not-so-subtle swipe in Landon's direction.

Teresa waited for an answer. Landon was not forthcoming.

"I'm sure that…" Cassie started but was stopped by Teresa's raised hand.

"Landon?"

"Teresa … er, Mrs Harkett."

"Landon," Teresa repeated, even more sternly. "You need to follow the syllabus in order for your students to do well in their exams. You're going off…"

"At a tangent? On a day trip? Like old cheese?"

"Off the syllabus," Teresa finished.

"It's all so stuffy. Dull, dull, dull. The kids don't want to know about the likes of Paradise Lost or Homer, they want to know all about Paradise City and Homer Simpson."

"A Guns & Roses song and American cartoon…" Cassie offered, smiling at Landon.

"I'm aware of The Simpsons," Teresa replied, then turned to Cassie. "But, thank you."

Cassie's smile faded.

Teresa turned back to Landon. "I think Cassie here has more literature running through her veins than you've got blood, including the syllabus."

"Hot dinners," Landon said, then frowned realising that didn't make sense. But then nor did the syllabus.

"They're bright children," Teresa continued.

Landon, more than anyone, knew that. "Yes, Teresa."

"So where are things going wrong?"

"Could you be a little more specific?"

"Do I really need to be?" she paused. "Okay, then. Grades. Let's start there."

"As good a place as any."

"You've seen them, Landon."

"I have."

"That wasn't a compliment." She paused again. "Well?"

"Bit of a cough actually, but thank you for–"

"I wasn't asking. The grades, they need to be improved and quickly, and I'm sorry…"

Landon and Cassie were pretty sure she wasn't particularly.

"You won't get the students where they need to be."

"I could hire a minibus," Landon offered.

"That's why I know you'll be the perfect person."

"But you just said…"

"Not for English literature, Mr Smith." At that point she knew she'd lost them. "You know Preston Grey?"

'Grey by name, grey by nature,' Landon was tempted to say but then thought better of it. "Preston, yes."

"I do too," Cassie piped up, wondering why she'd been invited.

"Yes, well, he's retiring."

*At last*, Cassie thought.

"Really, so soon?" Landon said.

"So," Teresa continued, "We'll need a replacement drama teacher and the school has no bigger drama qu– fan than you, Landon."

"Really?" Landon asked. "I thought you were going to…"

"Sack you?" Teresa shook her head.

"Really?" Landon asked, just to be sure.

"Absolutely. I've seen you with the children. They adore you. So do the staff, deep down. And some deeper than others," she said, turning to Cassie who blushed and looked down at her lap. "Landon, you just need to be doing something more… hands on."

Landon turned to Cassie, smirked, then looked back at Teresa. "Then I don't quite understand why…"

"I want Cassie here to take over your role."

Cassie looked as stunned as Landon.

"She's the obvious choice." Teresa confirmed.

"She is?"

"I am?"

"She knows her Shakespeare like the back of your hand."

Landon and Cassie exchanged uncomfortable glances.

"It's fine. Just keep it outside work. She's a great supply teacher, you could be a great teacher. You just need to be in the right place."

And for the first time in a long time, Landon knew exactly where that place should be.

## Death and Life

*Inspired by the photo 'Lunch atop a Skyscraper'*

### *Death*

*I wonder how long would it take me to reach the ground if I jumped?* Mario thinks as he swings his legs in the light breeze. *How many bones would I break? Which part of me would hit the sidewalk first?* He won't of course, would have thought about it a year or so ago but he's turning his life around, working hard, getting off the booze.

This is his last bottle of old JD. Mr Daniels and Mario go way back. JD was there when he needed him or thought he needed him but instead of going to the liquor store, he's started going to the café next door. Hadn't even noticed it before, in a world of his own, but it's real cute, a real homely atmosphere with damn fine cups of coffee.

He sits looking at his colleagues, eating their lunch next to him on the girder, chatting away, not a care in the world and thinks, *They're lucky – probably have swell homes, loving wives… gals who make their lunch pails and kiss them off to work. Someone to meet them, hold them, have their supper ready on the table when they get home, someone to care for them… think about them when they're not there.*

The 'old' him would have felt all bitter and twisted, but he takes a good hard look at them then at himself, and sees they're no different; just men trying to be happy, getting through life as best they can.

Things on the outside are improving too; the Depression's easing and the mayor's got big plans for the grand city of New York. "Do something about the smog," he says – breathe it in and it chokes you – gonna be a thing of the past. "Look to the future" he says.

More high-rise buildings as far as the eye can see, right up to the clear blue water of Rhode Island and out to Martha's Vineyard. So the city is on the up, literally, and that's gonna keep Mario in a job, so he's all for it. Maybe he'll even get out of the Bronx and move to Queens… and one day Manhattan!

So they're constructing the great Empire State Building. Making a new piece of history – John Raskob's vision – he reckons there'll be a million bricks by the time they've finished.

Had to be higher than Walt Chrysler's Building. *That Raskob fella must be mad*, Mario thinks, *doing all this just to outdo his rival. Hey, maybe one day I'll even be able to buy one of their cars.*

This girder is boiling – Mario feels like his arse is burning. Fred's got the right idea, bare chest and all.

Mario looks down, at all the people, the worker ants, crawling about their business, never talking to their neighbours. Up here, they're a world away. Mario then spots his apartment block. *Could do with a lick of paint.*

His mind wanders to the girl in the coffee shop yesterday, thinks maybe he'll speak to her tomorrow. "What? Yeah, Joe, it's a fantastic view. Thanks, I'd love a cheese sandwich."

***Life***

The hospital doors fly open and a woman is screaming out, "Where's my husband? Where's Charles?"

Twenty blocks away a man kneels down and takes a picture. Little does he know that this innocent snap will be famous worldwide for many years to come.

Right now he's thinking about getting the job done before he rushes home to his expectant wife. Their first child is due any day and he can't concentrate. So he continues staring through the viewfinder, hoping for clear shots before getting his equipment together and going home.

He looks at the people who compile his picture. Eleven ordinary men but with nerves of steel. He marvels at how they could sit on a tiny narrow ledge hundreds of feet up in the air.

He expects them to look fragile – as if a gust of wind could carry them over at any point – but they're as strong as the girder they sit on. His eye, then lens, focus on a solitary figure at the end.

Although he's sitting next to his colleagues, he seems detached – a bit of a loner – and a liquid lunch it would appear. Looks like he has the weight of the world on his shoulders. The photographer wonders what the man is thinking. He puts down his camera and sighs.

The heat of the day hits him. He had thought that it would be cold so high up but it's baking. The white vested guy manages to look cool, clearly used to the heat. Apart from the outsider, the rest of the group seem very relaxed.

One lights up a cigarette for a colleague, two others shut their lunchboxes and get to their feet and all but four head back to their site office, casually strolling back along the solid iron tightrope as if they were part of a trained circus.

The four remaining men chat for a while, then to the photographer's amazement, swing round to face each other and lay length ways along the girder and go to sleep!

He carefully takes more pictures - the shutter sounds deafening as it closes. Today has been one of the best of his life. How many people have the opportunity to see life so raw. Up, natural above the clouds?

He feels privileged. Here he is…over a thousand feet off the ground, witnessing the building of the eightieth floor of a planned one hundred and two. As he watches the men nap, he realises that he'll have little sleep from now on but he can't wait.

As his thoughts drift, his wife is going through the early stages of labour.

Senior nurse, Bertha Albright, applies a damp compress to her patient's forehead and holds her hand while a colleague tries, again, to get hold of the father-to-be, willing for the day when people will be able to carry telephones with them.

Bertha has assisted in numerous births but the moment a baby arrives still amazes her. She is sure that tonight would be no different.

A visitor in the next ward talks to her friend about a customer in her coffee shop the previous night and hopes that she sees him again before too long.

## Daphne The Tour Guide

Daphne slammed her clock card into the machine until she heard the metal stamp clunk. Easing it back out, she winced as she read the time, hoping that the clock above the machine was fast. 08:28.

Her boss Elijah didn't do late. Or at least it wasn't in his vocabulary, unless he was telling someone else off for being it. He'd have a field day with her today. Twenty-eight minutes. Half an hour, may as well have been half a day.

Like Daphne, Mark was invariably late but he'd get away with it because he was the boss' son. And neither of them could explain to Elijah that she should be let off because she was secretly dating said boss' son… and had been for three years.

They were surprised he'd not noticed the snatched glances in the dining hall, hands lingering when passing paperwork, the amount of times they were at the printer bank at the same time.

Late was late and that's all there was to it.

"Women should know better," Elijah had said to her once. She'd been on time for a long time after that but every now and then she just couldn't help it. And this morning couldn't be helped; dead battery in alarm clock, sun late waking her up.

No excuse really, but it wasn't as if she didn't make up for it with skipped lunches, often one of the last to leave. Not that he noticed those things, but at least she had a clear conscience.

That was until her colleague, accounts assistant Gilda, told her about her brother leaving his job as a tour guide for a belated gap year and how Daphne would be the perfect person to fill his shoes; with her knowledge of the town and soothing steady voice.

Torn between seeing less of Mark but being in a job she might actually enjoy, Daphne applied. 95% hoping 5% anticipating, she'd squealed as she'd received the call on her mobile a few evenings later, just as she'd been opening her front door.

Of course Elijah was not best pleased. "At least when you women get yourselves up the duff there's a chance of you coming back when you've had enough of the little ankle-biters. I knew there was something flighty about you, Daphne. Just up and leave at the first opportunity."

The first opportunity had taken fifteen years but that clearly didn't count. She wondered why his lovely wife Brenda put up with him.

The mixed feelings returned when she was thrown a surprise leaving party, with a table full of gifts – not one, she noticed, from Elijah.

Gilda had been right. She'd needed little training; sitting in on two different routes, she soon had it licked. A good memory had certainly helped; ever since she was a child she could glance at a shopping list and remember every item, which was how she'd ended up in accounts; a head for figures.

Financial statistics in the old job turned into dates and distances in the new, and she even threw in a few facts she'd already known.

As the open top bus drove past the old racecourse, she'd tell her clients, mostly foreign tourists, about its history dating back to 1632. The races had then stopped, due to accidents in 1681 until the then Lord Spencer (she soon learnt to pause at the mention of him for the 'oohs' and 'ahs' that proceeded) resumed them in 1727. A couple at the back looked particularly interested, and even stopped kissing when Gypsy Lane and Romany Pub were mentioned, before resuming their passionate embrace.

As the bus toured the town, she neglected to tell them of the seedier areas or aspects of its chequered history; one face for tourists, one for natives, although she did tell those with heartier constitutions that the racecourse, also known as Kingsley Park, had been used for public executions from 1715 until 1818.

The weeks flew by and Daphne began recognising familiar faces so she'd vary the talks she gave, feeling a bit like a stand-up comedian doing consecutive nights in one place.

Regular driver Stanley was also cheerful; whistling old tunes from 'On Top of Spaghetti' (one of Daphne's favourites) to, being a Cliff Richard fan, 'Living Doll' (to which Daphne used to mime the Young Ones' additions) and 'Summer Holiday', with some of the passengers joining in when they knew the words.

One afternoon, on a particularly sunny day, the double-decker was full except for two spaces at the front of the open-top balcony. Clicking the 'speak' button on her cordless intercom, she asked, "Are they definitely coming, Stan?"

"Yes, dear. The gentleman's checked in with me, he'll be up there in a second, says the lady's just parking the car."

"Okay, thanks."

Daphne stared at end of the bus until the man appeared. Another face she recognised except that instead of being a pleasant surprise, her stomach lurched. A blast from the past. The only compensation was that she'd be seeing his wife again.

Elijah hadn't noticed Daphne and it wasn't until he took his eyes off the stairs and around the bus that his smile turned to a gasp as he spotted her. His eyes then darted from her to the stairs and back again.

Daphne's attention also turned to the stairs and wasn't surprised, given his reaction, when it wasn't Brenda but a twenty-something brunette with a large chest and, as she walked towards Elijah, an equally large bottom; a figure not out of place in a Tomb Raider computer game.

With her advert-white teeth beaming, she clearly only had eyes for Elijah; contact-lens-blue eyes. Even though Daphne knew they'd checked in with Stan, she had the option, and therefore excuse, to ask for their tickets. As she approached Elijah, she noticed he was still holding them. Without speaking, Daphne smiled and looked at the tickets, then Elijah, whose mouth was still open.

"I think she wants the tickets, darling," the brunette said.

Saying nothing, Elijah handed them over.

Daphne smiled and handed them back before saying, "Thank you, sir. I'm afraid that we may have to curtail our tour a little today as we work to a schedule, although I'm sure we'll still cover all the major land…" she paused, "marks."

At the mention of his son's name, the colour drained from his face and he finally closed his mouth.

## Man Overboard

The crowds cheered as the ship left Southampton, relatives and friends waving from quayside to stern.

For Tina though, there was no one waving to her. Her only living relative had already gone to their cabin. To unpack, relax, watch TV, if there was one in the room. She'd forgotten to check when she'd booked, last minute, a Caribbean cruise to get him, Ronnie, off her back.

It had been his idea for a holiday, hers to take a cruise, knowing he hated planes. Hated anything that moved, so it had taken some persuading to get him here and that's why she'd left it late. So he'd have no choice. Turned it round so he'd thought it was his idea; he'd congratulated himself in the end.

Long after the passengers had gone to their rooms, Tina was still standing on the deck. She'd leave him as long as she could, hoping he'd be too engrossed in a political memoir or thriller to notice her absence. Save what little conversation they had left for another time.

Timing her return just short of the evening meal, he was already dressed in his dinner suit when she opened the cabin door. "You look smart, dear," she said, despite thinking it more appropriate for a funeral.

"You're late."

"Sorry, dear. I've been taking in the view. It's so–"

"You're going to get changed, aren't you?"

"Of course, dear."

"Well, hurry up."

"Yes, dear."

They took their places at a corner table, Ronnie choosing to be away from the other passengers. He hated crowds and even more so glaring lights. Tina would have rather been surrounded, even yearned to have been on the captain's table, to be part of the chatter, but knew what made for an easier life.

With so much food on offer, they were spoilt for choice although with Ronnie's gammy leg, Tina did all the choosing and carrying.

"Bit plain, this food," was his first response so she'd gone for something more interesting the second round. "You know I don't like spicy" then made her tone it down and by the time they'd had everything on offer, Ronnie one to get value for money, Tina noticed the room was almost empty.

"Nearly midnight," Ronnie announced.

"Is it, dear?" Tina asked, images of the dancing still playing round in her head. She'd liked to have joined in but she knew he would have refused and been even worse had someone else asked her. She'd had snippets of conversation at the buffet tables but then had to leave the talk half-finished when the plates were full.

"Come on then," he barked, and got up to return to their cabin, leaving a wake of plates scattered around the table, having been neglected by the waiters who'd been concentrating on the fuller parts of the room.

"Let's take a walk along the deck," she suggested, following Ronnie out of the large dining room.

"What for?"

"To get some fresh air."

"We live in the country, you're surrounded by fresh air."

"But this is the middle of the ocean."

"Exactly. Nothing to see. Besides, it's November. Too cold."

"Please, Ronnie. For me." She didn't play the 'for me' card very often because it didn't usually work but he must have been in the holiday mood because, although he sighed heavily, he veered away from the direction of the cabin corridors instead heading towards the outer deck.

Keeping close to the railing, Tina breathed in deeply. "Isn't this lovely, Ronnie?"

Ronnie grunted.

"Come look, Ronnie. At the sparkling water."

"You know I'm not keen on water and that I can't swim."

"It's alright, darling, there's a rail all round."

"Well…"

"No, Ronnie! No! Help! Please someone! Help!"

A middle-aged suited man ran to Tina as she peered over the edge. "Madam! What's the matter?"

"It's my husband! He's fallen in the water. Please, do something... please hurry."

The man leant over the side of the ship looking in every direction. "Are you sure, madam? I can't see anything."

"Please! You have to do something. He can't swim." Tina was sobbing.

The man dug in his pocket, pulled out a tissue which he gave to Tina then tapped some numbers into his mobile phone. "Marco Stephens here, I play the piano in the... yeah. There's a lady here on deck who says her husband's fallen over the side... Okay, thanks. At the back, by the tennis courts and... please, she'd doing her nut. Cheers."

Continuing to look out at sea and calling Ronnie's name, Tina wasn't paying much attention to what was happening behind her until she heard her name being called.

"Mrs Peters... Mrs Peters?"

Tina swung round. "Sorry?"

"I'm Captain McHugh. Mrs Peters, you say..."

"Yes, it's my husband. We were standing here, admiring the view when... he... He can't swim and he was looking down at the water when... I couldn't stop him... It all happened so quickly. Please, do something."

"I'm sorry, Mrs Peters, but... your husband, you say?"

"Yes. Ronnie."

"We don't have your husband listed on the ship's–"

"I remember you," a woman said from behind the captain. She stepped forward and looked at Tina. "We were chatting at the buffet table. You were filling two plates but then told me you were on the cruise alone, and that having two plates was force of habit. That your husband had died recently in a boating accident. That you hadn't adjusted yet and were still doing things as if he were still alive."

Silently, Tina nodded.

"There then," the captain said gently. "That explains it. You must have seen something that reminded you and... The mind can play tricks, you know."

Tina nodded again. "Thank you. You've been so kind. I'm just being a silly..."

"Nonsense," the pianist butted in. "It's quite understandable. It must be very raw."

Tina smiled weakly.

"Take her back to her cabin, will you…" the captain said to the pianist.

"Marco," Marco told him.

"Yes, thank you, Marco."

Turning back to Tina, the captain said, "And you must sit with me tomorrow evening."

"Thank you, that does sound lovely," Tina whispered.

The group dispersed and Marco walked Tina back to her cabin.

"Are you sure you'll be alright?" he asked as she put her key in the lock.

"I will, thank you. It'll just take a bit of time to get used to…"

Marco smiled, then continued down the corridor.

Tina went inside their… her cabin, and shut the door behind her.

Sitting on the end of the bed, she smiled as she looked at the array of beautiful dresses hanging in the wardrobe. Having chosen the simplest one for the first evening, she knew exactly which one she'd wear next.

## May The Fourth Be With You

"Half a pound?" Sonya looked into Wendy's eyes as the older woman wrote the figure on to Sonya's card.

"Well, yes, but half a pound is still progress. You've not gained so there's no dreaded circle on your card and you're only four pounds away from another silver star."

"But half a pound. I've been *so* good this week." To Sonya, shifting half a pound a week was as bad as not having lost anything. Five pounds in money to lose half a pound in weight, not exactly fair.

"Don't worry," Wendy soothed. "Everyone has weeks like this. Be just as good this week and you'll probably lose more next Monday night."

So Sonya had. Everything with more than a reasonable amount of fat went; her favourite crisps, no takeaways or ready meals, just meat, vegetables and fish. She was positively glowing with pride by the end of the weekend.

"Nothing! Seriously? Nothing?"

Wendy shook her head. "I'm sorry, Sonya, but I'm sure next week…"

Sonya took back her card when offered and rejoined the group. She sat in silence while Wendy gave her talk then traipsed back to her car.

Opening her front door, her tabby cat strolled to greet her.

"Nothing tonight, Buttons. Absolutely nothing!"

Taking that as lack of food, Buttons plodded back into the kitchen and out the cat flap, leaving Sonya to sit on the sofa and watch TV until it was time for bed. Buttons re-emerged, ate the offered food then joined Sonya upstairs.

As she walked home from work the next day, she went past, as she did every afternoon, Gregory's Bakery. Sitting solitary in the window, a pack of four Chelsea buns called her name. Sonya decided she'd be doing the shop a favour by buying them so they could close up and go home. So she handed over her

£1.50 and carried the bagged buns reverently out of the shop and towards the park.

Sitting on a bench by the lake, she carefully removed the pack, folded the paper bag and tucked it into her handbag. "Waste not want not," she said.

Pulling apart one of the sealed ends of the pack, she put her nose closely to the two buns nearest the opening and inhaled. Fruit and sugar. Sickly but heavenly.

She then stared at the buns. "I'm not going to eat you all." So pulling the biggest of the front two out of the plastic wrapper, she started stripping it into small pieces and threw them, one by one, into the water causing a rugby-type avine scrum.

Spotting a smaller bird missing out, she stood up, tucking the pack under her left arm and threw the remaining pieces of the first bun out to the runt which managed to devour some of it before being enveloped by its larger rivals.

With a smile, Sonya turned round to walk back to the bench when one of the handlebars of a bicycle bumped into her arm knocking the pack to the ground. The second bun flew out and landed on the grass by the bench.

"Watch out!" the cyclist yelled as he whizzed by.

All Sonya could do was growl at him as he disappeared into the distance.

"Never mind," she said to herself. "Two left. Two more than I should have but it's only Tuesday. I can work it off. Walk faster. Go the long way to and from work."

So grass-covered bun number two was ripped into shreds and went the same way as its predecessor.

Sitting down and facing the lake, she pulled out the third bun and was lifting it up to her mouth when she heard barking from her right. She turned round to see a particularly gorgeous-looking Jack Russell-cross heading in her direction. "Ahh…" she said, as it bounded towards her but then screamed as it leapt up at her, grabbing bun number three from her hand. "No!" she and the dog's owner shouted in unison.

"Lula!"

Sonya looked from her empty hand to the teenage girl who was trying to prise the bun from the dog's mouth.

"It's okay," Sonya said mournfully. "Let her have it. It's fine. I have another one."

The girl let go of the soggy bun and the dog trotted off, head held high, before slumping to the ground, releasing the bun and eating it at her leisure.

"I'm so sorry," the girl said. "I'd give you some money but I'm only here to walk the dog."

"It's fine, really. These things happen. I shouldn't be so greedy and if she's hungry then let her have it."

"Not really. She's just had her supper but 'an ever open door' as my mum says."

Lula then reappeared, licking her lips and nudged Sonya's empty right hand.

"Was that nice?" she asked the dog. Lula barked and walked back to the girl.

"Sorry, again," the girl said before putting Lula on her lead and walking her out of the park.

Sonya looked down at the bag containing the remaining bun. "At least I still have you. And only having you will taste all the sweeter."

She was then conscious of someone standing next to her; almost next to her, next to the bin, rooting through it. Staring at the dishevelled man Sonya guessed to be in his sixties, she looked at bun number four then back at the man. "Are you hungry?" she asked. "Sorry, silly question."

The man just stared back at her.

"Do you like…? Another silly question. Here…" Sonya offered him the final Chelsea bun.

With a whiter smile than Sonya had been expecting, the man took the bag, removed the bun from it and dropped the packet into the bin. Whispering a "thank you" before carefully unravelling the bun, he slowly put the first edge into his mouth and sighed, as if he could hardly remember the last time he'd tasted anything so good.

Sonya wanted to say something else to him but he turned and wandered off in the direction of the bandstand. She then spotted another man, similar in stature but slightly older, sitting on one of the concrete steps. The first man, with bun in hand, sat down next to his friend and peeled another edge from the bun, handing it to him and smiled as he ate it just as reverently.

Sonya watched as the two men finished the bun and sat chatting. Wishing she had something else to offer them, she got up and walked home.

The following Monday, as she stepped on the scales, she thought, *Please… another half-pound, half-pound, half-pound.*

"Four pounds! Well done, Sonya. Another silver star on your card."

Sonya beamed as the other women in the queue clapped and she thought, *Four pounds; one for each bun, and I don't miss them at all.*

## Petrified

The second time I met Phil Trollope, I was a completely different person. He'd obviously exhausted his luck up north so was trying his hand at the Home Counties, my Home Territory. Unfamiliar to him so for once I had the upper hand. And I made the most of it.

Having Tyler with me helped. It kept me level headed although he didn't take to him. Tyler to Phil. Dogs aren't stupid. I did meet a stupid greyhound once, dull as a ten-watt bulb, but Tyler's a full hundred-watt. Low energy but full power when it's needed.

And I found Phil's weakness. Dogs. Had always been scared of them. Petrified in fact and although Tyler is not much more than ankle height, he packs a mean punch, a hearty bite when given the right word. Trollope. Not just a coincidence. As I said, he's a clever dog.

Turns out Phil's car had broken down on the way to meet a woman in one of the villages just this side of Aylesbury and he'd got lost – followed the sat nav. I've been there before; not doing a U-turn in Uxbridge, but that's another story.

So there he was walking along the country lane in the middle of nowhere, the (stolen) VW flashing its little heart out a few yards down the road and what does he come across but a converted windmill. My windmill. It's the only building around and there's a light on, so he clicks the gate and walks up the needs-some-attention driveway before knocking on the door.

Tyler barks and while he normally barks at anything that catches his attention, it's not often that it's followed by him running to the front door.

We don't get many visitors – most people don't bother. It's either too far or they take one look at the shabby exterior and figure I don't have the money to want to buy whatever it is they're selling.

I was only in the kitchen so it didn't take me long to get to the door but long enough, I saw when I looked out the spy hole, for him to start walking away.

He was smartly dressed, expensive suit, not the average salesman, besides it was nearly eight o'clock, not the sort of hour for door-to-door knocking; they use the phone for that these days.

I opened the door and said "Hello?" loudly enough for him to hear, holding Tyler's collar.

Phil turned round and looked at the dog.

At this point, the normal thing would be for me to have said, "It's alright, he's harmless" but Tyler wasn't acting right so I hung fire.

I didn't recognise my visitor straight away but as he walked towards me, it didn't take long for that familiar feeling to return. Not hatred but anger. Anger that he'd taken advantage of me at my lowest.

He'd got a cut on his chin and I was looking at it as he reached the front door.

He put his hand up to the cut and rubbed it. "Shaving this morning, stupid really," he said, but I suspected a more dubious reason.

I smiled, despite it dawning on me who was standing there. "Can I help you?"

"Erm." He hesitated as Tyler gave a growl.

I smiled again and nodded as he looked up at me.

"I'm sorry to disturb you," Phil continued, his charm having not lost its touch. "My car broke down along the lane and I was wondering if I could borrow your landline – my mobile isn't picking up any signal."

"We are rather in the middle of nowhere. Sure, come in." It felt like inviting in a vampire.

Tyler gave another growl as Phil edged forward so I picked up the dog and stepped back, letting the blast from the past into my house.

He smiled as he walked and I smiled back but my smile was different to his. I knew neither was genuine – we both had agendas, but at least I knew that I had the upper hand.

I knew him from old and up to then, he'd not recognised me.

Even when we got inside and I shut the door (I'll tell you about the door in a minute) and started speaking, he didn't twig.

It took quite a while... in fact he didn't realise until I started reminding him about those years ago in a certain house in Northampstead, a pub near Wellingford, the refusal of entry, the hospital (cleverly disguised as a police cell) and so on. His face really was a picture – captured on my CCTV for posterity.

The door, yes, it's a clever piece of work. The internet is a wonderful place for information. You can do anything; build bombs, research books, change innocent-looking everyday objects into whatever you want them to be.

Like a simple plastic, uPVC door, into a fortress. It had to be plastic, couldn't be wood, holds the current better. More metal in it, more locking mechanisms and so on. Clever people on the world wide web.

So, there he was at my mercy. With only one exit in the building and that a one-way door unless you know the trick, I could take my time. He was already late for his date, he'd told me that pretty early on in our conversation, so I was doing her a favour by keeping him here.

I let him make the call in the end but it didn't go anywhere – the outgoing line's programmed to ring itself so he gave up after getting the continuous engaged tone after a few attempts. "No hurry," he said. I think he fancied his chances. I *am* female.

So I poured him a drink; strongest thing in the house – he was that kind of stupid too. Maybe he thought he'd be staying over. I did give him that impression. "I'd just made dinner," I said, "and there's plenty for two."

So he jumped at the offer, probably thought it would lead to another. We were having fun; the more he drank, the more relaxed he became. I didn't need to relax and he was miles ahead of me on that score.

He seemed to tire quickly too; strange that. He looked at the clock on the wall with hazy eyes; asked if that was the right time (it was) and if he should ring the breakdown company again (he could have tried but it wouldn't have got him very far).

I reminded him what they'd said (which was nothing but he didn't twig and couldn't remember) and he soon forgot what he was waiting for.

Waiting for most people is a horrible feeling. I have nothing I need to wait for anymore but it doesn't bother me. The British are famous for our queues and I use the time to people watch; it's amazing what information you can gather without anyone opening their mouths.

It's like that programme 'The Mentalist'. He can tell more about someone in the first five seconds than most people can after an evening's conversation. Patrick Jane, that was the guy.

I like making up words and ideas. I imagine the ideas fighting with each other in my brain; dip into the filing cabinet and duel with the folders containing all the other information that's in there. Some dustier than others – life part (a) and life part (b).

As I watched Phil fall asleep, I set my plan into action.

## The Threadbare Girl

It's the two clocks she finds the most comforting. Both beat a different tune, started with batteries within a few seconds of each other. Alternating like an analogue tennis match.

Of course she doesn't need two, it being such a small room and she's not going anywhere, so really she doesn't even need one. But they keep her company. The only noise in her existence. Except for people going to work, then home. Car doors, house doors, the shouting in between. There's no one for her to shout at. About. Not that she would anyway. She's too calm for that.

She only knows the seasons by the temperature of the room. With her body playing tricks on her, that's not even accurate. She hears the radiators kick in around the house but hers isn't working.

It's the sun she misses the most. She sees chinks of it but it's not the same. She can't see the whole; her favourite fruit, high up in the sky. Burning into the skins of those allowed out. Playing, talking, oblivious to the freedom they take for granted.

She's brought food every now and then, when he remembers. Sober enough to recall he's not alone.

For the first few weeks she thought she'd be rescued, familiar hands picking her up, arms wrapping round her like Christmas paper, but the stranger's arms have become familiar.

Sometimes she sits in the old empty bath; it cools her after he's been. She needs it sometimes more than others, depending on what he's expected of her.

She's thought about drowning, but water's a friend and a friend wouldn't do that to her. He tells her they're friends, special friends, and she smiles so he believes it. He's nicer to her when she smiles so it's an expression she's learned to wear, glued in place as soon as she hears footsteps.

He's told her his name is John but she doesn't think it's real. None of it is. It's a three-year-long dream that loving hands will wake her up from.

He buys her clothes, always a size too small like he wants her to stay a child, as does she. "They grow up so fast," her grandfather had said and when she sees him again she wants to be exactly the same. The tomboy who wouldn't be seen dead in pink, but now wonders if she will be.

Everything about the room is childlike, like it was bought with her in mind; pretty pictures, toys to play with – only they've never been touched. She wishes she were a toy.

Her smile snaps in place as the stairs creak. She hears the bolt and the door hinges complain. She'd tried that once.

Her smile's still in place as the arms reach out to her. She's frozen to the spot, near the bath, in her pink and purple cotton summer dress.

The hands recoil as they touch her skin as if electrocuted by the cold.

"Good god, Ajay!" The woman in the black trouser suit looked up at her colleague.

"You only need to look at her, Mandy, to know she's freezing," the older man added, scanning the room: a toilet, bath and cot, too small for a child her age. "Where's she been sleeping?"

"I'm not sure she has," Mandy replied.

Knowing how long the girl had been missing, Mandy battled with what to say to her. She wasn't trained for this.

As if reading her mind, Ajay crouched beside her.

The girl flinched.

"It's okay, love," Ajay whispered, stood up slowly and backed away.

Mandy looked at her. Her clothes, too sheer for the time of year, were threadbare like the room she'd been kept in. "Charlie, you're going to be fine. You're safe now." She knew that was the best thing to say. No point in asking her if she was alright. Even the strongest person in her position wouldn't be alright. And she looked as thin as a wafer and just as fragile.

"Where is he?" Charlie whispered.

Mandy looked at Ajay. He shrugged his shoulders. "We don't know," she answered honestly.

Charlie's eyes widened.

"It's okay, we have someone outside watching," Mandy lied.

Ajay looked at his watch. "We should be quick."

Charlie yelped.

"It's okay," Mandy repeated. "Take your time." She removed her jacket and went to put it round Charlie's shoulders but she recoiled. "Please," Mandy said softly. "You're cold. Too cold. This will make you feel better."

Those were words Charlie had heard before, many times. After *he* had been with her, he'd given her some hot chocolate and told her everything would be fine, *he'd* make her feel better.

She frowned. She did feel a little better; that it wasn't *him*, but she didn't know *them* either.

"Your parents sent us to find you, Charlie," Ajay said. "They're worried about you. They want you home."

Charlie shook her head. *He* had said that. That her parents had sent him to collect her from school. But he hadn't known her name. They knew her name. Her real name. She'd told him to call her Olivia, her sister. He'd said it was beautiful and he'd been happy.

But then he'd found out her real name and got angry. Beat her. But that was a long time ago and there was nothing to prove that now. No scars on the outside.

She closed her eyes and nodded. At least she'd be with a woman. And women didn't do bad things to little girls.

"Okay, let's go," Ajay said gently.

Mandy put her jacket around Charlie, it swamping her, then placed an arm around the girl's shoulders, and escorted her out of the cellar, following Ajay up the stairs, past the door with the squeaky hinges, into a kitchen Charlie had never seen.

She yelped again as the sunlight hit her eyes.

"Got your sunglasses on you, Mandy?" Ajay asked.

Mandy went to dip into her handbag.

"No, please," Charlie begged, releasing Mandy's grip. "I want to see it, to see it all. Where **he** lives, where I've been living for–"

"We'll talk about that later, Charlie," Ajay interrupted. "We just need to get you away."

Charlie stopped walking and stared at the hall they were now standing in, then back at the kitchen. Immaculate. It was all perfect. Her grandfather had called her 'immaculate'. Miss Perfection.

Then told her how her parents had waited so long to have her. Her and Olivia. The other half of her egg. That had made her laugh. She'd wanted to have eggs for breakfast for the rest of the week. Share them with Olivia. To make up for stealing her half before she was born.

Charlie had her back to the front door when they heard the key.

Mandy grabbed Charlie's hand and pulled her behind her, behind the front door as it opened, leaving the two men to stare at each other.

Ajay instinctively went for the inside of his jacket, for the gun that hadn't lain there for over ten years.

John's eyes followed Ajay's hand and he launched his bags of shopping at him, one of them knocking him off balance.

Charlie screamed and John swung round. "Olivia! What are you doing?"

Mandy, still obscuring most of Charlie, looked over at Ajay who nodded.

"John," Mandy said calmly, "Charlie needs to come with us."

"That's not Charlie!" he hissed. "She's Olivia."

"Okay, John," she said, despite knowing that not to be the case. "You need to let Olivia go, let her come with us."

"Never!" he snarled. "She's mine!"

With John distracted, Ajay crept up behind him until a floorboard in the nineteen thirties house gave him away and John twisted back round so the men's faces were inches apart.

Charlie tugged on Mandy's hand and took off the suit jacket. Remembering what he had done to her to get her there, Charlie whispered in Mandy's ear.

With the two men not moving, Mandy knew she had little time. She took the jacket and holding one shoulder in each fist, lunged at John throwing the jacket over his head, pressing down as hard as she could.

With John dropping to his knees, Ajay pounced, bearing down on him while Mandy retrieved the mobile phone from her handbag.

"Yes, hello. Police please, and ambulance. Twelve Atkinson Street. Please hurry. Thank you."

Charlie shivered as she leaned against the radiator, watching the two private detectives restrain the man she'd known as 'John', the man who'd been her father figure for the past three years, the 'best friend' in Olivia's absence, who'd made her hot chocolate not quite like her mother used to make it.

As the radiator kicked into life, she remembered what it felt like, to feel it as well as hear it, feel the warmth she'd been missing, inside and out.

## Norman The Conqueror

"Grandpa will be here soon. Are you ready?"

I nod. *Doesn't it look obvious?* I think. Jacket on, bag in my hand. But then that's my mum all over. Treating me as if I'm two, which I'm not. Old enough to make my own decisions, get myself ready.

"Okay, well," she continues, "are you sure you're going to be warm enough?'

With two layers bottom half, four top half, this is… to use one of my dad's phrases 'a redundant question'.

I nod again. The only question left is "Are you eating enough?" She says that to Nick, my older, freer, university-living brother.

"And make sure you eat enough."

There we go. I've officially been 'Nick'ed.

"He hasn't said where he's taking you."

She's still talking. I'm Lizzie by the way. English as English can be. That's our family. Elizabeth, me, named after the Queen and my dad's mother… or probably more likely my dad's mother then the Queen. I've never asked. I don't have any relatives called Nicholas so that must just be a name they both liked. Mum did say they picked things that could be shortened but still sound okay. Nothing to be laughed at. I'm not laughing.

Mum is Yvonne, Dad is Christopher and Gramps (or 'Grandpa' as mum always calls him when I'm around) is Norman. Mum says he was named after Norman the Conqueror but we've done him in history and as far as I know, our Norman has never conquered anything – made an impression, definitely. He can't fail to do that.

Gramps takes me out every other Saturday when Dad's working. I see him other times of course, but our Saturdays are… ours. Just the two of us. And the most fun I have all week. All fortnight. He comes over for tea twice a week and he's a different person. Mum's dad. Normal, still funny but quieter. Fits his conversations in with everyone else's. Keeps quiet when there's nothing to say. But on our Saturdays, he's who I think he really wants to be – who he is to me.

"He's here!" Mum shouts, and I fly out the door, slamming it behind me. I catch "And don't slam…" and smile, looping my bag over my head.

I'd forgotten about Gramps' new car; a bright red convertible Ford Ka, like Wayne Rooney's. This is my second trip in it and I imagine Mum behind the curtains tutting and saying, "Why he has something like that, I don't know. It's so impractical. You can only fit two people in it. And the colour… He's acting like someone half his age…"

And that's what I love about him. My parents act older and I don't want to get to their age without acting like mine. Okay, so backwards baseball cap is going a bit far. He only puts that on when we've left the street so there's no chance Mum can see him.

And he wears jeans. Not even Mum wears jeans. Not sure why, I've never asked her that either. I take after my dad, but he's at work all the time and really I'm closest to Gramps. He's the one who gets me. Nick sort of does but he's never here either. When he comes home he's out with his non-uni mates. And he's popular, so he's always out.

Gramps starts the conversation with school. Takes an interest in what I'm doing so I tell him about Kelly and Malachi but then he talks about my schoolwork and I figure Mum's asked him to say something. She's worried about me, he says. She doesn't need to be. I do alright. Nick's always been the bright one. I'll catch up.

Gramps never tells me where we're going. We've done all sorts. Started off with the normal things: Gulliver's Land, Wicksteed Park, Whipsnade Zoo, Willen Lakes, but then it got a bit more adventurous. More fun. Instead of walking round the lake or having a picnic by it, we went surfing on it, water skiing.

Can't do that now; it's all frozen over, not safe. Too cold to go somewhere outdoors, and on the ground of course; Gramps is afraid of heights. Even gets wobbly on the shopping centre escalators.

I think we're going to the cinema or maybe go-karting – we did that last time but he knows I don't mind doing things twice, like Mum's casserole on a Wednesday. We all know it's leftovers but it tastes fab anyway.

We're driving further than we normally do, and in the opposite direction; north… and fast. Easy, Gramps.

But he's laughing and he has such a funny laugh. It makes me giggle.

He takes off his baseball cap and I see a bald patch. He's got more hair than Dad and more grey. White actually. "Distinguished," Mavis says.

She lives next door to us and I think she's got a soft spot for Gramps. I'm pretty sure I see her curtains move when he drops me off. I should get him to stay, or invite her to supper in the week. I think they'd get on.

But on a Saturday he dashes off, says he's got things to do. It's the weekend, people are busy at the weekend, aren't they?

"M6, Gramps?"

"Yes, Lizzie, but not far. One junction, Rugby."

I can't think of anything to do at Rugby. Dad took us shopping there once.

"Are we going shopping?" I ask, disappointed.

"Just wait and see."

Mum says the same when I've got something right that's supposed to be a surprise. Otherwise she says 'no'.

I haven't brought much money with me. Mum usually gives me a little but forgot. I don't like to ask as I know we don't have much. I hear my parents talking about it. I think the university's expensive. More than Nick thinks.

Dad gave him a summer job last year but it's still Dad's money isn't it? He's got a factory making paper but it's not the sort of paper Nick can use at college or me at school so that doesn't help.

Gramps leaves the motorway and turns right, away from Rugby. Now I'm really confused. It's signposted Blaby which I think is a village so we can't be going shopping. It's not long before we turn right again and as I see a line of old planes ahead of us, it twigs what we're doing.

He's always loved Messerschmitts and Spitfires so we've come to watch them, and I'm thrilled. It's a bit cold for standing outside but maybe there's a room with a glass window.

We've seen them on TV. They're so graceful, like birds. We've been bird watching too, that was fun. Not as boring as you'd think. Gramps knows a lot of people so we had an expert tell us what was going on – nothing like the TV. So much more when it's real.

A man about Gramps' age greets us as we park the car. He introduces himself as Maverick and invites us up to his 'office', a glass room on top of the red brick building.

Dad and I watched 'Top Gun' at Christmas, which was funny as it wasn't a Christmas movie, and this man looks nothing like Tom Cruise.

Dad reads Lee Childs' books and we've had *that* discussion a few times. Me and Dad, not Lee and me. This Maverick looks more like Jack Reacher, or how everyone imagines him to be.

Maverick asks us if we'd like a drink and Gramps asks for two teas, strong as Jack Russell. Maverick laughs and I can't tell whether he knows that Gramps means his favourite cricketer or the dog.

One of Maverick's colleagues makes the drinks while we sit on two old leather chairs. I love the smell so breathe in as hard as I can.

"You're not getting a cold, are you?" Gramps asks.

"No," I say and point to the chair.

He smiles and explains it to Maverick who says, "Why do you think I wear one of these?" pointing to his old flying jacket. I hadn't really wondered, but okay.

I'd drunk my tea slower than Gramps but he's always had a… what is it, Mum…? Oh yes, cast-iron constitution.

Gramps and Maverick are chatting away so I don't feel in a hurry and I can't see any planes doing anything.

I've just finished my tea when Maverick turns to me. "Okay, miss, are you ready to go?"

"Already?" I ask.

"If you're fit."

"Um, I think so," I reply. I play netball and swim for the school but I'm not sure how fit he needs me to be to walk back to the car. He can see I'm disappointed and turns to Gramps. "You've not told her, have you?"

Gramps smiles.

Maverick looks back at me, steps forward and reaches out to take one of my hands. "Come with me, young lady."

I look at Gramps and he winks, so I hold out my right hand which Maverick takes and leads me back down the stairs. Down the stairs and not back to the car but towards a big metal shed.

I turn back to look at Gramps and he catches up and holds my other hand.

As we walk into the first building, I see the most beautiful thing. It reminds me of the noughts and crosses board Gramps and I often play, only this one is bright red and white.

"It's a Tiger Moth," Gramps says.

I stare up at him. "Am I?"

He nods.

I scream, jump up and down like a pogo stick, clap my hands wildly then throw my arms around him. He laughs which makes me scream again and he puts his hands over his ears. He's so funny.

"Would you like to go first or second?" Maverick asks.

I turn round to him, puzzled. "Before or after who?"

He laughs. "Your grandfather."

I look back at Gramps. "But you're afraid…"

He gulps, smiles a little, then bursts into giggles.

Then I realise that he is Norman the Conqueror after all.

## A Military Couple

Laura watches the ship leave. Silence. No waving hands, no kisses blown. The major's words replay in her head. "He didn't tell you?" He hadn't. Not like him.

Laura pictures the box of his letters at the bottom of her wardrobe, at their home. The photos of him, comrades, even an ice cream van. She'd squinted at the face holding… no, offering the Flake ninety-nine. Offering it to him. Laura's husband.

Laura's never been the jealous type. Never needed to be. Until now.

It's the woman's brown eyes – like a puppy's. Alton's always been a sucker for those.

It had been her, Laura, who'd prevented them getting a dog. She loved them as much as he did but sneezed just passing one in the street. Every time she saw newspaper articles of sniffer dogs she'd smile, knowing they kept him company when she couldn't. But now he has this woman keeping him company. Surrounded by deep brown eyes whose owners know how to use them.

And now he'd made the choice. Home to her or stay with them. He'd written so freely, so lovingly that it had never dawned on Laura that there would be a choice. Could be. She'd stood with the other wives, waving, cheering. Except the other wives were holding hands with their children, until their husbands arrived and they let go, threw their arms around them. A group hug. A human parcel of flesh and blood.

She'd watched them one by one, group by group, get into their cars, and drive back to their houses, safe within the confines of the base. A bricks and mortar group hug. To homemade food, parties, reunions. Laura's still waiting for hers.

She doesn't mind it getting dark. It's the warmth she misses. A sunny early May day turned into a cold May night. She zips her jacket up to her chin and digs her hands into her pockets. She isn't sure why she waits; she knows there won't be another ship. Unlike buses, they don't come in threes. They come in ones and her one, his one, came and went hours ago.

She hears footsteps behind her and turns. A man in uniform and she nods.

"I'm sorry, ma'am. I'm going to have to lock up now. Do you have a ride?"

She nods again and walks to her car. It's still the one he bought her when they were first married but it drives well and she doesn't want to change it. She doesn't want anything to change.

The car starts first time and purrs like a kitten. The talked-about kitten that went the way of the dog. She drives the half hour to their detached redbrick house and pulls up to curtained windows with no lights behind.

Locking the car, she walks up to the green metal post-box, finds the smallest key on the ring and opens the door. It squeaks as she pulls it and she makes a mental note to locate some WD40. Alton would have noticed it before now and she'd never have known.

Picking out the solitary letter she recognises everything about it; the envelope, the writing, even the smell. She shuts the door and lets herself into the house.

Putting a pre-prepared casserole-for-two into the oven, she sits at the kitchen table and stares at the letter. She has twenty minutes to decide what to do. She can wait while she eats but she doesn't want to spill anything on it. She thinks about the dinner and what she's to do with the other half.

There's no dog to feed it to. Once it's cooked it can't be re-frozen so decides it'll keep in the fridge until it's binned or eaten. She knows it won't taste the same; eating alone never does. Conversations turn to silence as she has nothing to share.

The timer pings as the doorbell goes and she stares at one then the other. The dinner, too hot, can wait a while but with no one else it can be, she knows the other choice can't.

She runs to the door. He's changed his mind. Only when she opens the door, there's not one man to greet her but two. One takes off his hat, followed by the other. One goes to speak but can't find the words.

She knows him, from Alton's thirtieth. Ford, she thinks his name his. She recognises the other from earlier in the day and feels sorry for him, that he's had to leave his family so soon after getting home.

She knows why they're there so she doesn't need them to say anything. She knows she doesn't want them to speak but that they inevitably will.

"Wait," she says and the men look at each other. "Please come in and wait. Don't say anything. I need to do something first."

The men do as she asks, wiping their feet on the mat, although they all know there's not a speck of dirt to be found. They stand, caps under their arms, a gentle pressure that ensures no dents. They watch her walk into the kitchen, slowly as if stopping time. The men smell the food and Ford licks his lips then bows his head.

She sits at the table, holds the envelope in both hands then turns it over and opens it, pulling out the cream matt paper.

*My darling Laura. I have to keep this short as we're about to go on manoeuvres but I know you'll understand. Do you remember Ford from my birthday party? No, probably not. Too many faces, names. I'll send a picture next time.*

*His wife's due to give birth shortly and he won't be home in time. He didn't ask. He wouldn't, but I knew and... I'm sorry, really I am. I know you're going to be disappointed, but you'd do the same. I know you would.*

*Anyway, things out here are fine. We even have British ice cream. Not quite the taste I remember without you sharing, but it's a little piece of home. A little piece of you. Take care, my darling, and I'll be with you before you know it. Love always. Al xx*

Laura stares at the kisses and pictures his face; smiling, laughing, no fear in his eyes. The eyes, brown as a puppy's.

She stands up, places the letter into her pocket and walks back into the hall.

So she was there. Laura. I wish I'd looked harder now. If I'd known he hadn't phoned her, had sent a letter that hadn't reached her, I'd have found her, gone over, and said something. Invited her to ours.

Only I saw Ivy and little Daisy from the ship and well, I couldn't take my eyes off them and was oblivious to my surroundings. Which is not what we're trained to do but you don't expect to be looking for anyone else at something like that, do you? The crowd was just that, a crowd. Sure, I'd spotted other women I recognised but once I'd seen Ivy, that was it. Focused. Honed in. Homed in.

Guilty? Yes, very. I should have looked for her. Laura. To tell her. But I didn't know. And I know what you're thinking; that it's my fault he was out there. You're not wrong. I said I could wait. That she'd send me photos.

Wouldn't miss much, Daisy being so young and all, but Alton insisted. He was like that. Said he wouldn't miss much either, but I knew that wasn't true. He'd been out there longer than me but he loved it. Loved her of course too, but work was his obsession. It's the adrenalin. Unless you're in a job like ours, you can't understand.

He left before I woke up so I didn't get to say "goodbye". That's the worst bit. I wanted to say "goodbye", and "thank you". Again. He said once was enough but I don't think he knew how much it had meant to me. Means to me.

Okay, so he didn't give his life for me, as such, but if he hadn't have… no, I know. You can never tell. He could have had Plan A; seen her, returned out there and then… only they would have had that time, wouldn't they?

The time that Ivy and I are having, will have. For a month anyway. Yeah, she's scared. She always has been, will be, but doesn't say anything. I can see it in her eyes though.

The green eyes that said "Could have been you," when I told her the news. Before Laura. I'm sorry for that too.

A wife should always be the first person to find out. Nearer the top than someone she briefly met at a birthday party.

It was terrible, breaking the news. She knew it though, as soon as she opened the door. Invited Mick and I to come in but not to say anything. I couldn't anyway. Done it before but it wasn't the same.

Had to leave it to Mick. He was more professional about the whole thing. Detached. Not really known Alton. Not like I did.

I asked her if she wanted us to phone anyone but she shook her head. I don't know who she has now but admin will sort that out. Help her.

Send a woman to sit with her, give her someone experienced to talk with. They're better at dealing with that kind of thing.

Women. Except Ivy, but then she's bound to be emotional, with Daisy and that.

And Laura? Don't know. She comes across as strong, independent. I think she'll be fine… in time. And that's what it's all about, isn't it? Time.

You get used to waiting in our profession. Them here, us out there in a strange country that becomes familiar. They wait for us to come home, we wait at home to go back.

It's deathly quiet wherever you are and if you get used to that, then that's half the battle, isn't it?

## We All Have to Start Somewhere

Unless you were an expert, there was really no way of telling it was a forgery. In fact two experts had cleared it as genuine, although Natalie suspected that at least one of them had been paid off.

Peering at the right-hand corner of the canvas, she noticed a tiny speck that didn't look right, just below the 'Vermeer' signature. Usually it was the signatures that were the giveaways, however hard a forger practiced they didn't have the same 'sweep of the hand' as Nat liked to call it.

This speck looked too red, like the colours hadn't been blended well enough. It was possible that Vermeer had been sloppy, this was a newly-discovered work after all, but she knew, and adored, the rest of his pieces well enough to know a genuine from this.

"Still convinced it isn't real?" Smarmy Simon sneered as he walked past Nat's desk.

"Yep," she said confidently.

She watched him head out the office, and stuck her tongue out at his back.

Her colleague, Polly, gasped. "Nat!"

"He drives me nuts!"

"He drives us all nuts."

"He didn't see me."

"No, but what if he'd–"

"He was leaving."

"He could have turned round."

"Then I'd have pretended to lick my lips or something."

"And make him twice as obnoxious."

"Alright then, I could have pretended I had a crumb at the corner of my mouth."

"And make him think you eat while handling multi-million pound artefacts."

"Point taken, although this isn't one of them. You've not been here as long as I have, Polly. You'll be doing the same in a year or so. What have you got there?"

Polly held up a gold-coloured bracelet. “Supposed to be Cleopatra’s.”

Nat didn’t look impressed.

“It looks real,” Polly chirped.

“In your ‘expert’ opinion? Or your ‘wishing it were true’ opinion?” Nat, being paid to validate authenticity, always suspected a piece was a fake until she could prove otherwise. These days with modern technologies, they were getting more fakes through the doors then originals and she blamed the economy.

“I can’t find any flaws,” Polly said, less enthusiastically.

“How many pieces have we got to do?”

Polly looked at a list lying on her desk. “Thirty-two.”

“Oh, great. A week and a bit to validate thirty-two of the world’s most expensive… sorry, potentially the world’s most expensive and rare items. Even if we have sixteen each, it’ll be pushing it – it can take me a day just to do one. Take this Vermeer for instance, I’ve got to inspect every brush stroke…”

“Vermeer. Isn’t he the ‘Girl with the Pearl Earring’ guy?”

Nat laughed. “That ‘guy’, yes.”

“So that must be worth a fortune!”

“‘The Girl with the Pearl Earring’ yes. This one, not a lot.”

Polly screwed up her face. “Oh.”

“Yes, sadly, ‘Oh’.”

“Buy not a lot, you mean…”

“We can’t sell it as a genuine so the owner has a choice. It’s still worth something as a painting so he could still sell it but declare that it’s a like-for-like.”

“He can do that?”

“He can but he probably won’t.”

“Why not?”

“Because he’ll take it somewhere else, to a lower-profile auction house, where they don’t check so thoroughly, find someone who will say it’s genuine.”

“And someone will?”

“If he looks in the right places.”

“You said he has two choices.”

"Yes. The other is to take it home and hang it above his fireplace."

"He won't do that."

"Exactly."

"So he's a crook," Polly said wide-eyed.

"I don't know with this one. Not met him."

"Either way, it's a shame about his painting."

"There is a third option."

Polly grinned. "There is?"

"Oh yes. He could find an employee who's a little… shall we say, dodgy."

"Who?"

Nat's eyes looked in the direction of the doorway.

"No!" Polly said, genuinely shocked.

Nat nodded.

"Simon?"

Nat nodded again. "I'm not saying he is up to no good but can you explain the new car?"

"He was promoted when Victor left."

"Vic never earned that much."

"I don't know then."

"Maybe a long lost aunt."

"Do you think?"

"No, Polly, I don't think."

"But you don't think…"

"Yes, Polly, I do think."

"But…"

"Just look at him."

"Huh?"

"Don't you think he overcompensates for something?"

"He's just…"

"Yes?"

"Extroverted?"

"Overcompensating."

Nat carried on working on the painting as Polly stared at the door, waiting for Simon to return, not knowing he'd gone for the day. Gone to meet a new client, one with a very expensive vase, Ming possibly, though Nat suspected that when it came to her… Polly was still too new and inexperienced… that he'd also be sorely disappointed.

"Yes, sorry, Simon. It's most definitely a fake."

"You are sure?"

"Absolutely, no doubt about it."

"What am I going to tell Mr Jeffries?"

"Would you like me to?"

"Would you? No, I should do it… I am the manager after all."

"You are, Simon, but at least if I can explain to him the flaws… he's bound to ask you anyway, isn't he?"

"We'll both go."

"He might get angry."

"Do you think?"

"Oh, absolutely."

"Then I should definitely go."

"But he's less likely to get angry if there's just me. You know, he'll not want to lose control in front of a woman."

Simon looked into the reflection of the photo frame on his desk – the one everyone thought contained his wife and children but was his sister and his nieces. The sister he'd lost contact with since she married the actor and moved to London, a seven-hour journey from Edinburgh.

He thought then that maybe he should make more of an effort. "Okay then you go. I'll get a security guard to help you take the picture."

"Why?"

"Because..." Simon rubbed his chin. "Of course. What are they protecting? It's worthless."

"Not worthless."

"But you said…"

"Oh, it's a fake alright but it's a genuine fake."

Simon pushed his glasses up to his eyebrows and wrinkled his nose.

Nat continued. "It's probably worth a thousand tops. It's well done, but certainly no Vermeer."

"A thousand?"

Nat nodded. "Tops. You interested?"

"Never liked the thing. The old boy's welcome to it. Obviously thought it would provide him with a retirement nest egg. Buy a big yacht somewhere hot and surround himself with silicone blondes. Dirty old git."

"We could still sell it… declaring it a like-for-like, of course."

"Oh God no. Wouldn't give it catalogue room."

"But you were going to when you thought it was real."

"Of course, Natalie. We have shareholders to think about."

"Sure. So I'm okay to take it to him now?"

"Please. Get rid. Burn it, ship it off out Outer Mongolia, if you like. We get a nice fat fee anyway for your time spent, probably leaving the old boy enough to buy a boat for his bath if he's lucky."

"Poor man."

"Poor man, my arse. He's so loaded already. Didn't bat an eyelid when he bought it last year."

"Do you know what he paid for it?"

Simon burst out laughing. "I remember very well because he couldn't stop bragging about it. Wish I could see the look on his face when you tell him."

"And he paid…?"

"Oh yes. Seventeen million. Seventeen million! I ask you, who pays that for a thing like this."

"A Vermeer lover, I suppose."

Simon laughed again. "Only his good stuff. Like that girl with the blue hat."

Nat resisted correcting him, knowing it would only wind him up. "Is our client local?"

"Not far, in the big posh house over in Ravelston. Here. Got his business card. Or what he pretends to be anyway. Importer / exporter. Dodgiest of the dodgy." Simon handed over the card.

Nat looked at it and smiled. "Yes, I know where that is. I'll give him a ring and arrange to take it back."

"Great. Sooner rather than later though, yeah?"

"Sure. Definitely sooner."

"Good afternoon… oh, Mr Jeffries." Nat smiled as the man of the house opened the door, having expected there to be a butler or assistant of some kind. "Thank you for seeing me on such short notice."

"You brought it back," he said pointing towards the wrapped painting resting against one of the old pale stone entrance pillars.

"I'm afraid so, Mr Jeffries."

"Not worth anything, is it."

Nat shook her head. "I'm sorry, not really."

"Where are my manners? Come in, girl. You must be getting cold."

"Thank you."

As Nat stepped over the threshold, she struggled to take in the opulence of the place. Everything before her, she could tell at a glance, was as real as she was.

"Firewood value then, is it?" Mr Jeffries asked, deflated.

"Not really, I'd say about a thousand as a like-for-like."

"You're still willing to sell it?"

"Unfortunately not, I'm sorry. We only have limited space in the catalogue."

"I've been debating ever since I got the thing what to do with it. You see, I had my suspicions. I knew I bought it too cheaply and…"

"Too cheaply?"

"Not as it turns out. If it had been real, I'd have had to pay twice as much. Almost. Around the thirty mark, I'd say. I'd not seen it before but I could tell it was his… not one of his best, granted but a Vermeer through and through, but as we both know it wasn't to be. So it could go as a like-for-like, can it? Tell people it's not real and…"

"We can, Mr Jeffries, but I'm afraid…"

"Catalogue space. Yes, I quite understand. You see, I'd just taken over the house and contents from my father and I thought I was doing something wonderful by buying this… adding to his collection… an unknown Vermeer. I'm just glad he didn't live to see… Does this mean there's an original out there somewhere?"

"I'm sure there is, sir."

"Cain, please."

"I'm sure there is… Cain. I wonder…" she continued.

"Yes?"

"No, it's silly really."

"What, dear?"

"Actually I think it's probably unethical."

"That… sounds intriguing."

"I've sort of grown attached to it, having spent so much time on it, I suppose, and I wonder if… I have some money put by."

"Nonsense, dear."

"Of course. It's a shock, and you wouldn't want to part with it having bought it for so much."

"Oh no, dear. I don't want it. And I certainly don't want any of your money for it. You'd be doing me a favour actually. Having it around reminds me what I spent on it. Would you take it away?"

Nat nodded cautiously, successfully hiding her enthusiasm. "If you're sure."

"Oh absolutely. I liked it when I first saw it but… the tarnish has gone off it a bit. Do you know what I mean?"

Nat knew exactly what he meant. Like her falling for Simon's charms when she first arrived at the auction house, even being one of his conquests for a while, but she'd learned to put on an act. She did it all the time now, and, she thought, was really quite good at it.

She thanked Cain as she left the house, bubble-wrapped picture under her arm. As she drove back to her one-bedroom flat, on the wrong side of the city, she imagined her future: the boat, the blondes, only hers would be natural… genuine… Swedes called Erik or German Wolfgang.

This was her first con but as Cain's grandfather had probably told Cain's father, 'We all have to start somewhere' and where else to start but the top?

## Note from the Author

Thank you for purchasing 'Shorts'.

I hope you enjoyed these stories and welcome feedback. You can either find me through the links on the next page or via email: morgen@morgenbailey.com.

If you'd like to keep updated with my news, do subscribe to my monthly newsletter at https://morgenbailey.com/newsletter.

## About the Author

Morgen Bailey
Author of fiction & non-fiction. Editor.
Ghostwriter. Mentor. Speaker.
www.morgenbailey.com

Apart from writing, Morgen is also a speaker, mentor, tutor & lecturer of writing courses as well as a judge of writing competitions. She is an editor for publishers and indie authors, and offers a ghostwriting service.

As a former columnist for Writers' Forum magazine 'Competitive Edge' and chair of three writing groups, Morgen has judged the Flash 500, H.E. Bates, BBC Radio 2, BeaconLit, and Althorp Literary Festival short story competitions as well as the RONE novel competition. She also runs her own monthly 100-word competition.

Talks and workshops have included for the W.I., U3A, Troubador's Self-Publishing Conference, Delapré Book Festival, and NAWG Fest with her 'Editing your Fiction' weekend residential course.

Morgen can be found on Twitter, Facebook, and Instagram.

# Titles by Morgen Bailey

## Fiction

After Jessica — money and a girl gone missing
Hitman Sam — a trainee hitman and love triangle
One for the Road — a hit-and-not-run novel
Oh, Henry — a comic dog-detective*
Henry Short Stories – comic dog-detective shorts*
The Serial Dater — 31 dates in 31 days*
The Serial Dieter — 31 dishes in 31 days*
*published as Rachel Cavanagh

*Short Story Collections*
Shorts — a collection of short short stories
Flashes — a collection of shorter short stories

## Non-Fiction

*Morgen Bailey's Creative Writing Workbooks*

Writer's Block Workbooks
1000+ exercises and 50+ tips per book

Editing Fiction ~ A Writer's Guide
Morgen's guide to writing a story then pulling it apart